W9-BEX-500

Don't Drop Dead Tomorrow

ALSO BY HUGH PENTECOST

Pierre Chambrun Mystery Novels:

John Jericho Mystery Novels:

A Collection of Short Stories:

Don't Drop Dead Tomorrow

HUGH PENTECOST

A Red Badge Novel of Suspense

DODD, MEAD & COMPANY
NEW YORK

ISBN 0-396-06389-6
Library of Congress Catalog Card Number: 79-163073
Printed in the United States of America
by Vail-Ballou Press, Inc., Binghamton, N. Y.

Part 1

"I have a question for you, Mr. Quist," Colonel Brownlow said. He was a big man, over six feet, overweight, conservative in his expensive suit but flamboyant in his manner. He was very British. He was probably in his early seventies. He was having steak and kidney pie for lunch. "My question is this, sir. Do you ever do it upsidedown?"

Julian Quist leaned back in his chair, a faint smile moving the corners of his mouth. He was tall, slim, blond, half the colonel's age. He wore his hair on the long side, but very carefully arranged by his barber, known as a hair stylist in this age, who charged twenty-five dollars a visit. Quist's double-breasted blue linen suit with bell-bottomed trousers, his dark tan shirt, his orange tie, were eye-catching and extremely "mod." He held a very long, very thin cigar between his manicured fingers. His manner was languid, gently cynical. His pale blue eyes regarded Colonel Brownlow with mild amusement.

"I'm afraid you'll have to try again, Colonel," he said. "There are things I've done upsidedown, but I'm not sure what you have in mind."

"Your job, sir," the Colonel said. "You are a public relations expert. Your skills are used to build people up; make them look glamorous, lovable, honest—whatever is required to suit the situation. Have you ever done just the reverse: pulled someone down, destroyed his reputation, made him hated and mistrusted?"

They were lunching at Willard's Backyard, an elegant restaurant in New York's East Fifties. For a warm summer day like this one there was an awning-covered garden area, with flowers, shrubs, and two or three small trees. Quist's lunch, as always, had consisted of a ham sandwich and a pint of champagne. He turned the cigar around in his fingers, smiling at the Colonel.

"Are you offering to pay me to destroy someone and at the same time build you up, Colonel?" he asked.

"Damn me! To hell with me!" the Colonel said. "Have you read my book?"

"I'm afraid not. I didn't know you were an author."

The Colonel picked up an attaché case beside his chair and opened it. From it he took a book in a plain blue jacket. He handed it across the table to Quist. The title of the book was: *My Love Affair With a Queen.*

"Provocative title," Quist said.

He opened the book and found a frontispiece photograph of a giant ship. She was the *Queen Alexandria,* last of the great luxury ocean liners.

"Making her final voyage this week," Colonel Brownlow said. "I was her military commandant for four years during World War Two. By God, I love her. Always will."

"Not as sexy as I'd hoped," Quist said, handing back the book. "I've lunched with you, Colonel, because Bobby Hilliard said you were a great guy and needed the kind of help I'm equipped to give. Suppose we get down to it."

"Trying to, dammit," the Colonel said. "How would you like to see your old family home, place where you grew up, turned into a house of ill repute?"

4

"You do have a gift for odd questions, Colonel."

"We may have shortened World War Two by a couple of years, the *Alexandria,* the *Elizabeth,* and the *Mary,*" the Colonel said. "Stripped down to be a military transport each one of 'em could carry twelve to fifteen thousand men, each voyage. Outrun submarines. Outrun sea raiders. No escort. Damned wonderful old girls. Gallant, by God."

"Is someone suggesting the *Alexandria* be turned into a house of ill repute, Colonel?" Quist asked.

"You might say so," the Colonel said. "You might just bloody well say so!"

Quist's eyes danced. "You want me to build her reputation in this new capacity?"

"Not a joke, Mr. Quist. No joke at all." Brownlow drew a deep breath. "Luxury passenger service by sea has had its day, sir. Four and a half days to cross the Atlantic was a miracle in my time. Jet planes make that seem like crawling. Everyone in such a bloody hurry. So, when the old girl puts into port at the end of this trip she goes under the hammer. She'll be sold to the highest bidder. I represent a bidding group."

Quist leaned forward, tipping the ash of his cigar. "To turn her into a joy ship, Colonel?"

"Good God no!" Brownlow exploded. "She is history, sir, a landmark. She should be treasured. We see her as a museum celebrating the great days of luxury travel by sea, climaxed by heroic service in the great war."

"Support by private capital?"

"And by admission fees paid by the millions of people who will certainly want to see her and her historical mementos."

"So what *is* your problem, Colonel?" Quist sipped the last of his champagne.

"Other bidders!" the Colonel said. He sounded indignant. "One other bloody bidder in particular."

"What kind of money are we talking about, Colonel?"

"Seven, eight, ten million to buy. Fifteen to twenty million to refurbish."

Quist whistled. "You can put up that kind of bread, Colonel? I've been treating you with less than the respect due you."

"Respect my foot. I haven't asked for respect, sir. I'm here to discuss one other bidder with you. There are two. There's a group, about in the same financial position as my chaps, who want to make a floating university of the old girl. Respectable, at least. I think we might outbid them. But the other bidder is—well, sir, have you ever heard of a man named Jeremy Trail?"

Quist's eyes narrowed. "Oh, brother!" he said.

"You have heard of him, Mr. Quist?"

"Of course."

"Who is he?"

Quist studied the end of his cigar. "He is reputed to be the richest man in the world," he said. "They say he owns half the oil in the world. They say he owns three airlines. They say he owns most of the action at Monte Carlo, and most of Las Vegas that Howard Hughes doesn't own. Not too long ago he was rumored to be out to crush the Hughes interest. Munitions, ships. His enemies have accused him of being up to there in the drug traffic. Real estate. He is said to own the best part of everything that's worth owning."

"You ever see him?" Colonel Brownlow asked.

"No. He's married to a startlingly beautiful girl, an Italian princess, I believe. She does New York about once a year, but Trail seems not to come here with her."

The Colonel's dark eyes were fixed on Quist. "You know anyone who has ever seen Trail?"

"Offhand I can't think of anyone," Quist said. "But there must be people in the set who entertain Mrs. Trail here— she was the Princess Sophia Pravelli, if I remember cor-

6

rectly—who must know Trail."

"Care to bet? the Colonel asked.

"It would seem a fairly safe bet," Quist said.

"I'll bet you a thousand against your agreement to do the job I ask you that you can't find anyone in New York who has ever met Jeremy Trail," the Colonel said.

"And what exactly is the job you want me to do?"

"Sell the idea that the *Alexandria* should become a historical monument, belonging to all the people of all the world. And persuade the Whitehall Company that it would be criminal for them to sell the old girl to Jeremy Trail."

"The Whitehall Company owns the ship?"

"They do. They are an extremely conservative, old-world sort of company. My kind of world. If they knew the *Alexandria* was to be used to promote crime and vice and God knows what else, they wouldn't sell to Trail. They'd sink her first. But they have to be convinced. You see how it is, Mr. Quist. Trail, if he chooses, can outbid us, whatever we offer."

"And what makes you think Trail wants to use the *Alexandria* for criminal purposes?" Quist asked.

"No one can be that rich and be honest," the Colonel said.

Quist laughed. "I admit the ethics involved in acquiring great wealth may be questionable, Colonel. But to suggest that Jeremy Trail is a criminal is, I'm afraid, simply a clue to your natural feeling of frustration."

The Colonel moistened his thick lips. "As military commandant of the *Alexandria* during the war I was a sort of ambassador-at-large for Great Britain. We carried many VIPs as well as troops. I acted as host to kings, and prime ministers, and presidents, and famous journalists, and movie stars; all kinds of people who moved in the highest circles socially and politically. I've maintained a lot of those contacts since the war. Would you believe me if I told you that

I've never come across anyone who's actually met Jeremy Trail?"

"A rather remarkable coincidence, but a coincidence, Colonel."

"Would you like to know what I think?"

"Be fascinated."

The Colonel leaned forward, his voice lowered to a conspiratorial level. "I don't believe there is, or ever has been, any such person as Jeremy Trail."

"Wow!" Quist said, still smiling.

"I think Jeremy Trail is the invention of a group of international criminals. They hide behind this man who never was. Call them the Syndicate, the Mafia, or any other name you choose. Maybe more powerful than either of those groups."

"And his wife?"

"Another part of an invention for the public," the Colonel said.

"Look here, Colonel," Quist said, "that's a pretty wild idea. To prove it what you need is a first-class private investigator."

"No use," the Colonel said. "The Trail Interests could buy anyone like that I hired."

"And you don't think I could be bought?"

"I have been led to believe, sir, that you could not," the Colonel said.

Quist laughed again. "Flattery might just get you a boy," he said. His laugh faded and his eyes narrowed. "If you happen to be right about all this, Colonel, and what you call the Trail Interests discovered that I could not be bought, the next possibility is not very inviting."

"I believe the American phrase is 'a contract would be issued for a hit,'" the Colonel said. "You could be assassinated."

"Yet you suggest I take the job?"

8

"You are said to be a very clever man, Mr. Quist. One hopes you would be clever enough to keep them from knowing what you are up to. I certainly hope it because if it became known I was involved in exposing this fraud I might very well lie beside you in the morgue."

Quist's cigar had gone out. He dropped it in the ash tray. "I can't remember a more fascinating luncheon, Colonel," he said. "You'll have to give me a day or two to think about it."

"Time is of the essence," the Colonel said. "The Board of Directors of the Whitehall Company will sell the *Alexandria* to the highest bidder, unless otherwise convinced, within the next two weeks."

"We haven't discussed a fee," Quist said.

"When you decide to say 'yes' you write a figure on a piece of paper and that will be it," the Colonel said.

"And all this to insure the existence of a nautical museum," Quist said.

"I love that old girl, sir," the Colonel said. "I, by God, truly love her."

The offices of Julian Quist Associates were located in a glass-and-steel finger pointing to the sky above Grand Central Station. The offices were as mod as the gaudy clothing of their proprietor. The colors were pale pastels. The furniture was deceptive; the far-out designs augured discomfort until you sat down and were pleasantly surprised. Just as Julian Quist was seldom seen wearing the same suit twice in the same season, the office furnishings were constantly being changed, as were the paintings on the walls. On the afternoon of Quist's luncheon with Colonel Winston Brownlow the paintings in the reception room were a Reuben Tam, a Larry Rivers, and one of Churck Hinman's shaped canvases.

Miss Gloria Chard, the dazzling receptionist wearing her usual simple little Rudi Gernreich creation, sat in the middle of her circular desk juggling two telephones when Quist appeared.

"Lord, am I glad to see you, Mr. Quist," she said. "There are at least ten urgent telephone messages on your desk, and three of your top clients are waiting for you in the visitors' lounge."

"I'm not in, darling," Quist said. "I may not be in the rest of the day. Tell Dan Garvey and Lydia Morton I want to see them."

"But what do I tell people?"

"You are mystified. You have no idea why I haven't come back. They can always talk to Bobby Hilliard."

"No one wants to talk to anyone but you, Mr. Quist."

"Alas! Get Dan and Lydia on the double, my pet."

As Quist opened the door to his private office another door at the far end of the room opened and Miss Constance Parmalee, his private secretary, stood there. She was a thin girl with a good figure, red hair, and the proper legs for a miniskirt. She wore amber-tinted granny glasses that shaded very bright, inquisitive hazel eyes.

"I'm out for the afternoon, darling," Quist said. "You and Bobby try to quiet the cannibals in the visitors' lounge. I won't be available before tomorrow."

"Senator Kramer is most insistent," Miss Parmalee said. "He needs a special splurge before he addresses the United Nations day after tomorrow."

"You and Bobby can handle that," Quist said. He smiled. "You want a new fur coat for fall?"

"Of course," Miss Parmalee said, without blinking.

"Then keep me undisturbed except for Dan and Lydia. If I take on a certain new client you may be able to have a muff to go with it."

"Muffs are out of style," Miss Parmalee said.

"You are just the one to bring them back in, Constance. Be a lamb and split, will you?"

Miss Parmalee evaporated. Quist went over to a closet in the corner and hung his jacket there. He stopped by a wall bookcase and transported a *Who's Who*, a *Social Register*, and a *Celebrity Guide* to his flat-topped desk.

He had just had time to take one of his long thin cigars from a cedar-lined box on his desk and flip on his silver desk lighter when Dan Garvey appeared.

Garvey was the complete physical opposite of Quist: dark, brooding, conservative as to clothes. Ten years ago he had been a promising professional football player, the possessor of a Phi Beta Kappa key that he kept hidden. He was handsome enough to have made it in films if he hadn't gone to work for Julian Quist Associates after a knee injury had ended his athletic career prematurely. He was a primary target for the glamorous young women who staffed Quist's office, but if he had made a choice it was a secret he had kept extraordinarily well.

The office betting was that if Garvey had made a choice it was the exotic-looking Lydia Morton. Lydia Morton was always so perfectly turned out that she would have been taken for a high-fashion model rather than a gifted writer and researcher for the top public relations firm in the country. She was dark, sultry, with always the faint suggestion that she was troubled by some unsatisfied hunger. If the office rumor about Garvey and Lydia was correct it seemed odd she should appear unsatisfied.

"Hi, children," Quist said, as Lydia joined him and Garvey. He pushed away the *Who's Who* he had been studying. "Jeremy Trail, please."

"Oil, airlines, gambling concessions, munitions, real estate, shipping interests, possibly some high-level criminal associations," Garvey said.

"Married to the Princess Sophia Pravelli," Lydia said, "owns an island in the Mediterranean, gives fabulous parties in Monte Carlo, Las Vegas, Paris, Antibes, and on his yacht. Can buy and sell governments. No children—that is, legitimate children. Reputed to be handsome, vigorous, devastatingly charming."

"So what's new?" Quist said, turning his cigar slowly around in his fingers.

"What do you want to know, Julian?" Lydia asked.

12

"Friends?"

"He must have thousands of them," Lydia said, "at least in a social sense."

"Name one," Quist said.

Lydia's violet eyes widened. "Well, offhand—"

"Not offhand," Quist said.

"Literally thousands of people have been guests at his parties and on his yacht."

"Does Trail attend those parties in person?"

"Well, I suppose he does, Julian."

"Suppose me no supposes, darling," Quist said. He was smiling, but there was a curiously hard look to his face.

"Stop beating around the bush, Julian," Garvey said. "What do you want to know?"

"For openers, what does he look like?" Quist asked.

Lydia and Garvey exchanged puzzled glances.

"I've told you he is reputed to be handsome, charming—" Lydia said.

"Blond, brunet, or redhead?" Quist asked.

"I—I don't know."

"Some enterprising photographer must have gotten a picture of him at some time or other."

Garvey was scowling. "I've heard he has a thing about photographers," he said.

"I remember a picture of him," Lydia said. "He was coming off his yacht somewhere, surrounded by his entourage."

"So what does he look like, love?" Quist asked.

"It wasn't a good picture. He was wearing an overcoat, collar turned up, hat pulled down over his forehead, dark glasses," Lydia said.

"Could have been Dan," Quist said.

"What the hell are you getting at, Julian?" Garvey asked. He sounded irritated.

Quist took a deep pull at his cigar. "Let me tell you about a luncheon I've just had with a rather engaging elderly Brit-

13

ish colonel," he said.

He told them. When he came to Brownlow's theory that Jeremy Trail didn't exist he saw a look of total disbelief on both their faces.

"Your colonel is off his ever-loving rocker," Garvey said.

Quist glanced at Lydia, but she had no comment.

"Trail's listed in *Who's Who*," Quist said, indicating the open volume on his desk, "but it's a very incomplete listing. Nothing about his parents. Nothing about his education. Nothing to indicate his age. Only a long list of the many companies of which he is a director. He's not the president of anything, or the treasurer of anything. He holds no office that would require his presence, say, at an annual meeting."

Garvey picked up the *Who's Who* and glared at it.

"On the surface it should be fairly simple, Lydia," Quist said. "You have an in with all the gals who cover society doings here in New York for the media. It shouldn't be difficult to find out who Mrs. Trail's friends are when she's in town. Some one of those people who are her intimates must have met Trail—if he exists."

"Are you really buying that possibility, Julian, that he doesn't exist?" Lydia asked. There was a thin frown between her lovely eyes.

"My elderly colonel has sprinkled me with itching powder," Quist said. "I hoped you and Dan could cure that itch by telling me you'd seen Trail somewhere, or naming some chum of his. You haven't. So see if you can't dig up a cure for me, children."

Garvey slammed the *Who's Who* shut. "It's too wild to make any sense," he said. "But suppose it's true? Why in God's name should you get mixed up in it?"

Quist watched the smoke curl up from his cigar. "You've been with me long enough, Dan, to know that curiosity about people is a kind of disease with me. As a public relations man I've spent most of my adult life building up

14

façades for people and businesses, more often than not phony. What really lies behind those façades, whether I created them or they're just homemade, fascinates me."

Garvey made an angry gesture. "Like the man said, a contract could be issued for a hit. Crook or no crook, Jeremy Trail isn't the kind of man who would hesitate to slap down anyone who started nosing around in his affairs or invading his privacy."

"If he exists," Quist said, smiling.

"If he doesn't exist—which I still say is a wild idea—then you're sticking your neck out in a situation you can't handle. Trail Enterprises has the power to knock over governments. One successful public relations genius with an office full of sexy dolls and an ex-football player with a gimpy knee would be child's play for them. Oh, they don't have to kill you, Julian. They just have to pass the word and you won't have a client left, a business left. That's how they'll handle it."

"I resent that kind of power," Quist said.

"I resent not eating," Garvey said, "which is what'll happen to me if you persist in being curious."

Quist smiled, but his eyes were cold as two newly minted dimes. "So find me someone who has met Trail, talked to him, knows he exists, and I'll forget about him."

"So it could take a couple of days," Garvey said.

"I have a couple of days, Daniel."

"If we can't find anyone?" Lydia asked, her eyes wide.

"Then I have to make a decision, don't I?" Quist said.

CHAPTER THREE

Dan Garvey was an impatient man. When he was on a job he liked to be direct and quick about it. He hadn't beaten around a bush in years. When he wanted a woman he asked for her. No charades. When he wanted facts for Julian Quist he went to the horse's mouth and not to the stableboy.

Finding out the truth about Jeremy Trail was not a new kind of job for Garvey. The Seeker Of Truth they called him in the office. Julian Quist might use his talents and those of his staff to build an elaborate false front for a client, but one requirement, as far as Quist was concerned, was that he must know the truth. It was important for him to know what he had to hide and on what he could build. Quist pretended to a kind of cynicism about his job. He pretended he didn't care how much of a sonofabitch a client was provided he, Quist, didn't look like a fool for taking him on. The truth was he cared quite a lot. Garvey's findings had resulted in Quist's turning away dozens of apparently highly respectable clients. It was this deep-down integrity of Quist's that kept Garvey working for him.

But Garvey was angry about the Trail assignment. Trail wasn't a prospective client. Julian was fooling around with a buzz saw. Julian had no right, Garvey told himself, to jeopardize himself, his staff, and his business just because he was curious. Julian's crazy colonel had opened up a particularly poisonous can of peas.

That afternoon Garvey was confident it wouldn't be too difficult to find someone who had, at one time or another, shared a martini with Jeremy Trail. Garvey's horse's mouth in this case was one Terry Baldwin. Terry Baldwin was a fabulously rich young man who, among other things, was perhaps the best amateur squash-racquets player in the country. He traveled with a very fancy crowd, spent a part of each winter on the Riviera, owned an apartment in Monte Carlo, and had almost certainly rubbed elbows with the people who rubbed elbows with the Trails. Terry's father had owned a piece of the professional football team on which Garvey had been a star performer some years ago. Garvey had been a sort of hero to the then teenaged Terry. When Terry was in New York he always looked up Garvey. Just two nights ago they had done the town together.

When he was in town Terry Baldwin worked out with the racquets pro at the Athletic Club each afternoon. That was where Garvey found him. Terry had finished his game, had his steam bath and massage, and was sitting in the locker room, a towel around his neck, sipping a tall glass of orange juice. There was a bottle of gin on the table beside the juice glass.

"Sweat the stuff out of your system and then promptly refill," Terry said. "What cooks, chum?" His sleek body was well muscled.

"I need a small piece of information," Garvey said.

"It's yours if I have it," Terry said.

"What kind of a guy is Jeremy Trail?" Garvey asked.

Terry laughed. He wiped his face with an end of his towel. "The Shah of Persia," he said. "He owns everything worth owning: islands, yachts, gambling casinos, and the most beautiful woman in the occidental world. You want to float a loan?"

"I know how rich he is, and how powerful he is, but what's he like?" Garvey asked. "Don't I recall you visited his island a couple of winters ago?"

"I did, and came away so shattered from coveting his wife that I still haven't recovered."

"But what's Trail like?"

"Most fabulous host in history," Terry said.

"Old? Young?"

Terry grinned at Garvey. "With that kind of a woman he can't be too old, man. She needs caring for and she seems happy."

"For God's sake, Terry, tell me about Trail."

"All I know is rumor," Terry said.

"You visited his island and you don't know him?"

"Never laid eyes on him," Terry said. "He was away on some kind of business junket the week I spent there."

"And you've never met him anywhere else?"

Terry shook his head. "And thought I was lucky at the time. Gave me the opportunity to work my charms on Sophia. She's the most beautiful of all women. I couldn't budge her, which makes me think—vain as it may sound—that Uncle Jeremy is quite a guy."

A muscle rippled along the line of Garvey's jaw. "What would you say if I suggested that he's a myth, doesn't exist?"

Terry laughed. "I would say you were off your chump."

"Introduce me to someone who knows him personally," Garvey said.

"Why not?" Terry said. "Fellow named Felix Hargrove is president of one of Trail's oil companies. He was just here. If you'll wait till I put on some clothes, we may find him downstairs in the bar. I heard him say he was dining here."

Felix Hargrove was in the bar. He was a man in his middle fifties, had avoided a middle-aged pot, looked sun-lamp healthy. He was relaxed and socially charming.

"You used to be a fullback on the Hawks, didn't you, Garvey?" he said, when Terry introduced them. "You gave me quite a few thrills, my friend. Drink?"

"No thank you, sir," Garvey said. "But you can help me win a bet."

"Do my best," Hargrove said.

"I have a friend who has bet me I can't find anyone who knows Jeremy Trail personally."

Garvey could have sworn that Hargrove's genial smile was abruptly frozen. "Well, you win your bet, Mr. Garvey. Jeremy is a business associate of mine. Of course I know him."

"Then he's not a myth, Felix?" Terry asked.

Hargrove's pale eyes didn't leave Garvey's face. "Of course he's not a myth. Is that what your betting friend thinks, Mr. Garvey?"

"So few people seem ever to have met him face to face," Garvey said. "Terry here visited his island, for example, and never met him."

Hargrove's face had turned hard and hostile. "You are an example, Mr. Garvey, of why Jeremy stays out of the public eye as completely as he can. Everyone is curious about him. Everyone wants to get at him for help, or to sell him something. Are you selling something, Mr. Garvey?"

Garvey tried to laugh it off. "Of course not, sir," he said. "I just wanted to win a bet and you've helped me do it."

"You can be assured that Jeremy Trail is very real," Hargrove said. "And now, if you'll both excuse me—"

Myra Rudolph wrote a syndicated column about society with a capital S. She had made herself a rich woman by exploiting a talent for laughing at the Very Rich and the Very Beautiful, sometimes good-humoredly, sometimes with the devastating effect of a dentist's drill on an exposed nerve.

19

She had a value to the lesser lights because she reported their presences at the Right Parties. She was the darling of the people in the world of High Fashion because she described the clothes the Very Beautiful wore at those Right Parties. Myra had made and destroyed young designers in the field. Myra, apparently, was invited everywhere that the Very Rich and the Very Beautiful congregated. She was feared by them, but she was also needed by them. If nobody reported their Doings—I mean, what's the point?

Myra had been a blonde, a brunette, and a redhead at various times. Her clothes were sensationally "of the moment" because she got them free from the In Designers. She had a good figure and calculating green eyes. In public she was rarely seen without some eligible young bachelor in the Very Beautiful set, but rarely the same one twice. Men appeared to be a kind of window dressing rather than a serious Life Work.

Myra Rudolph owed Lydia Morton a favor or two. Lydia had put her on the track of some rather special scoops relating to clients of Julian Quist Associates.

About the time that Dan Garvey was talking to a suddenly unfriendly Felix Hargrove, Lydia and Myra Rudolph were having cocktails at a corner table at the Café Renaissance on East Forty-ninth Street. Myra had made a note or two, congratulated the maître d' on the excellence of the martinis, and passed along a choice bit of gossip about a Washington hostess who was said to have embarrassed the President no end.

"You didn't invite me here just because you love me, darling," Myra finally said to Lydia. "Tell me, is it true what they say about you and Julian Quist?"

Lydia's face was suddenly expressionless. "What do they say?"

"That you are desperately in love with him, darling, and that he may be just a little bit queer?"

20

"You know you just invented that," Lydia said.

"Is it true that Julian has a hundred forty-six suits in the clothes closets in his apartment?"

"I have never been in his clothes closets," Lydia said, trying to curb her anger. She didn't want to start this with a row.

"All right, darling. Have it your way. So we are here for what reason?"

"Tell me about Jeremy Trail. You do know him, don't you, Myra?"

"Of course I know him," Myra said. Her eyes were turned toward the entrance where someone was waving at her. "I interviewed him not too long ago."

"Perfect," Lydia said. "Tell me when the interview appeared and I'll run it down. I'm anxious to find proof that someone has seen Trail and talked to him."

Myra looked down at the twist of lemon in her martini glass. "I'm afraid you'll have to take my word for it," she said. "The interview was never published."

"Pressure from Trail?"

Myra looked uncomfortable. "You might say so," she said.

"When and where did you see him?" Lydia asked.

Myra gestured to a hovering waiter for a refill. "You do know that I'm very much in Sophia Trail's good books," she said. "I always see her when she comes to town. She always manages to find time to invite me for a little private chit-chat. As a matter of fact I'm lunching with her day after tomorrow. She's coming in from Southampton on the last voyage of the *Queen Alexandria*."

"And you met Trail through her?" Lydia asked.

Myra waited until her empty glass had been removed. "Look, darling, you and I have always leveled with each other, right?"

"Right."

"If anyone in the world asked me if I know Jeremy Trail I

21

would, of course, say 'yes.' I do know Sophia. I have talked to her endlessly about her husband. But I'll tell you the truth if you'll promise never to let it leak."

"What truth, Myra?"

"I've never laid eyes on Jeremy Trail," Myra said. "He never comes to New York with Sophia. I once attended a big party he gave for Bardot in Paris, but he didn't show up personally. He is my one defeat, darling. It is the passion of my life to be the reporter who finally breaks through the barricades and gets an interview with him. But I think you can understand why I'd never admit in public that I've been unable to reach him. I once got to Howard Hughes, you know, but this man is even tougher to approach."

Lydia felt a cold finger running down her spine. "Has it ever occurred to you, Myra, that Jeremy Trail doesn't exist?"

"My dear girl!" Myra said. "What a sensational idea!"

"We have a new client—a Colonel Brownlow who used to be the military commandant on the *Queen Alexandria* and who knows everyone—who swears Trail doesn't exist, that he's never come across anyone who's actually met him. Of course it's an absurd idea. Your Sophia must have talked to you about her husband."

"Oh, Sophia is passionate about him," Myra said. "He must be something for her to resist all the men who flock around her. A Greek god, from her description. A pirate, right out of a seventeenth-century romance. Tender, tough. Every woman's dream—according to Sophia."

"She's shown you pictures of him, I suppose?"

Myra shook her head. "He has some sort of phobia about cameras," she said. "He's determined to stay as anonymous as he can. If people knew what he looked like, he'd never be able to walk down the street of any city without being mobbed. The tantalizing thing about it is I may have seen him a dozen times and not known it. But your idea is truly

22

sensational, darling."

"That he's not for real?"

Myra's green eyes were bright. "Suppose I were to circulate that rumor! He'd have to see me then, wouldn't he, to stop the gossip? No, no, Lydia, I'll take the check. You've given me a brilliant idea!"

Julian Quist's apartment was a duplex on Beekman Place. There was a terrace outside the living room which overlooked the East River. On that particular summer evening Quist was sitting by himself on the terrace, watching the slow-moving lights on the water's surface. On a glass-topped table beside his wicker chair was a tall glass of Rhine wine and soda, frosty with shaved ice. He was smoking one of his thin cigars, experimenting with smoke rings. His father had been able to blow them perfectly, one after another. Quist had never met with that kind of success.

The doorbell rang. Quist got up and went through the living room to answer it. There were only four people who ever got as far as his front door without being challenged in the building lobby. Dan Garvey and Lydia Morton, two of them, were together when Quist opened the door.

"We met in the lobby," Lydia said.

"Bursting with information, I trust," Quist said.

Garvey was frowning. He headed for the bar in the corner of the room without waiting for an invitation. He poured himself a Jack Daniels on the rocks. "Scotch?" he asked Lydia.

"Please, Dan." She followed Quist out onto the terrace. As she passed him to take the chair facing his her hand touched his hand quite casually. "I almost didn't come," she said.

"Oh?" Quist stretched out in his chair and reached for his drink.

"I spent an hour with Myra Rudolph," Lydia said.

"What fun for you."

"She's really not so bad when she stops play-acting," Lydia said. "At any rate, she told me the truth, which wasn't helpful. She knows Sophia Trail quite well, but she's never met Trail. He doesn't come to New York with his wife. Myra's attended at least one of his big parties in Paris, but Trail didn't put in an appearance. She tells people that she's met him, interviewed him, but she hasn't. I suggested to her that perhaps he doesn't exist. She doesn't believe that for an instant, but she thinks if she circulates the rumor it might bring him out into the open—at least for an interview with her."

Quist frowned at his cigar smoke.

"One piece of information that may be useful," Lydia said. "By coincidence—or maybe not—Sophia Trail is arriving in New York day after tomorrow on the *Queen Alexandria*. Apparently a lot of famous people are making that last crossing on the old ship. Sentimental journey."

"And you haven't made up your mind?" Quist asked.

"According to Myra, Sophia Trail talks endlessly about her husband. According to Myra, Sophia describes him as a romantic and exciting gent."

"According to Terry Baldwin, Sophia is the most beautiful woman alive," Garvey said. He came out onto the terrace and handed Lydia a Scotch on the rocks.

Quist turned his head. "But Terry hasn't met Trail?"

"Nope," Garvey said. "Spent a week on Trail's island and fell in love with Trail's wife, but not Trail. However, I did meet a business partner of Trail's who knows him personally and intimately—he says."

"That satisfy you, Daniel?"

"No, goddammit, it didn't," Garvey said. He moved a third chair as though he was angry with it and sat down. "You know, Julian, when I left your office this afternoon I thought this whole notion was a lot of B.S. It wasn't until I met Mr. Felix Hargrove, president of one of Trail's companies, who claims to know him well, that I began to think there might be something to it."

"That doesn't make sense, Dan," Lydia said.

"I know it. But Hargrove didn't laugh when I suggested it; instead he got mad and brushed me off. That's when I began to wonder."

Quist smiled at the end of his cigar. "Curiouser and curiouser," he said.

"Something stinks about this, Julian. Stay out of it," Garvey said.

Quist looked lazily down at the river. "It's wonderfully farfetched," he said. "I wonder what the lady would say if it was put to her?"

"The lady?"

"Sophia Trail."

"Myra says—"

"To hell with what Myra says." Quist stood up and walked over to the terrace wall. He turned back to look at his two friends. "I'd like to put it to her in person and see how she reacts. Not what she says, but how she looks."

Garvey finished his drink and stood up. "I've got one other angle," he said. "George Forrest. He's a Government lawyer who tried an antitrust suit against the Trail Interests a couple of years back. It seems unlikely that he or someone from his office didn't get to see or talk to Trail. Anyhow he'd have a solid reaction to the suggestion that Trail doesn't exist."

"As I recall it, Forrest lost his suit," Quist says.

"Which doesn't mean he didn't examine the Trail world from top to bottom. I'll feel better if I can find George before I go to bed. I'll let you know what he has to say."

Garvey walked out and the front door opened and was firmly closed.

Quist sat down again. Across from him Lydia turned her

25

head to one side and removed one of the silver-and-lapis ear buttons she was wearing. Then the other one. She juggled them in one hand. Then she stood up and went over to Quist. She turned her back to him.

"There's a little hook-and-eye thing at the top of this dress. Would you undo it for me, Julian?"

Quist stood up. His fingers seemed practiced. Lydia started to laugh.

"So what's funny?" Quist asked.

"Myra," Lydia said. "You'll never guess what she asked me."

"So I won't try."

"She asked if it was true that I am desperately in love with you and that, unfortunately, you are a little queer."

"Bitch," Quist said, cheerfully. "There you are, my love, all unhooked-and-eyed."

"She also wanted to know if it was true that you have a hundred and forty-six suits."

"A hundred and fifty-three, counting dinner jackets," Quist said.

Lydia crossed to the living room door. Her violet eyes were very bright. "Hurry, darling," she said.

CHAPTER FOUR

Colonel Winston Brownlow was seated at a round table in the bar of The Players, a club founded in the last century by that great American actor, Edwin Booth, for his fellow actors, artists, writers, and others affiliated with the theatre or patrons of the arts. A little bald man was screaming insults at the Colonel, and the Colonel was bellowing back profane retorts. Quist, standing in the entrance to the room, was smiling. Here were two men obviously very fond of each other. Quist edged his way past the pool table where other insults were being traded and approached the Colonel.

"Ah, there you are, Quist!" the Colonel said. "I hesitate to introduce you to this disreputable character, but—Jack Worthington, Julian Quist."

"All I can say for you, Quist," the little man said, "you don't keep very good company."

"Screw off, you little jerk!" the Colonel shouted. Then, as Worthington walked away, pretending huff, the Colonel chuckled. "Lovely fellow. Dear fellow," he said. "Sit down, Quist. What kind of a drink will you have? I'm delighted to see you've made up your mind in only one day."

"Scotch on the rocks," Quist said, "and I haven't made up

my mind. But perhaps you can help me do just that!"

"Scotch on the rocks for my guest, Richard!" the Colonel shouted at the bartender. "And the usual for me." He looked like an eager bulldog. "I can tell by looking at you, Quist. You haven't found anyone who knows Trail. Right?"

"I've found someone who says he knows Trail," Quist said. "One of my associates found him, but he doesn't believe him."

"Fine!"

"Tomorrow about midday the *Queen Alexandria* is due to dock in New York," Quist said.

"Don't I know it. Time's running out, Quist."

"Did you also know that among the passengers is Mrs. Jeremy Trail?"

"I know," the Colonel said, his face turning glum. "A lot of Trail people on board, licking their lips in anticipation. Bastards!"

"You must have friends at the Whitehall Company."

"Of course I do. Good friends."

"Would it seem unusual for you to feel nostalgic and to ask a favor?"

The Colonel cocked his head. "What sort of favor?"

"Would it seem unreasonable for you to ask permission to meet the *Alexandria* on the pilot boat, bringing a couple of friends with you? You'd have a last hour on the old ship."

"There's to be a big party aboard when she docks," the Colonel said. "I was, of course, going to that. Old friends aboard to say goodbye to. But—I think I might manage the pilot boat thing."

"I'd like to talk to Mrs. Trail in casual surroundings," Quist said. "Everybody will be talking to everybody on the old ship. She won't think it odd to find herself talking to a stranger under the circumstances."

"By God!" the Colonel said. He stood up, like a volcano erupting. "Let me make a phone call."

28

The bartender had brought drinks, and Quist sipped his Scotch. Jack Worthington approached him. "Wonderful old boy," he said, nodding toward the phone booth into which the Colonel had wedged himself. "You help him, Quist. The *Queen* means a lot to him."

"You know what he wants me to do?" Quist asked.

"Of course I do. Old boy's my best friend. You can count on it he's right, you know. Couldn't be a Jeremy Trail. No man can stay hidden without a single soul knowing him— not and run the world. Depend on it, he's a myth. You help Brownlow. He shouldn't have to lose his ship."

The Colonel's influence with the Whitehall Company proved to be all that Quist could have hoped for. It was arranged that the Colonel and two guests should join the pilot boat the next morning on its way out to Ambrose Light and a meeting with the incoming *Alexandria*.

"What friend you bringing?" the Colonel asked.

"A very charming young lady named Lydia Morton," Quist said. "She's one of my assistants. There may be people in the Trail entourage who'll gossip more readily to a gal than they will to me."

"You can bring a geiger counter," the Colonel said, "and you still won't come up with Jeremy Trail."

Quist strolled into his office a little after three that afternoon. Miss Gloria Chard, her usual high-fashion perfection, greeted him with her usual wail that there were people waiting to see him, urgent and demanding phone messages.

"And Dan Garvey has a Mr. Forrest in his office. I was to let him know the moment you came in, Mr. Quist."

"I'll see them now, love," Quist said.

"And the people in the visitors' lounge?"

"You will charm them; you will turn those who will be turned over to Bobby Hilliard; you will say I have the Asian flu, which is a forty-eight-hour flattener."

Miss Constance Parmalee popped out of her private cubicle and stood at attention when Quist entered his office. She must have had a dozen messages for Quist, but she never delivered a message until she was asked if there were any. She wasn't asked on this occasion.

"Constance, my love, we do have some sort of connection with Jud Walker's office, don't we?" Quist asked.

Jud Walker was the mayor's official city greeter.

"Jud Walker owes you his left arm," Miss Parmalee said. "You helped make him an institution."

"Give him a call for me. There's to be a big party aboard the *Queen Alexandria* when she docks at Pier Ninety-one sometime around one o'clock tomorrow. I want invitations for you and Bobby Hilliard."

Miss Parmalee's eyes were expressionless behind her granny glasses. "Why are we going?" she asked.

"Lydia and I will be coming in on the ship," Quist said. "We're going out on the pilot boat to join her at Ambrose Light. I want you and Bobby there in case I need you."

"To do what?"

"I don't honestly know; won't until the time comes. Wear your best midday bib and tucker, darling."

The private door to the office opened and Dan Garvey came in accompanied by a scholarly-looking man, turned out by Brooks Brothers; about forty, Quist guessed.

"I mentioned George Forrest to you last night, Julian," Garvey said.

Forrest had a firm handshake. He was clearly surprised by Quist's double-breasted pink linen suit with its large black buttons. He tried to hide his reaction by starting to fill a Dunhill pipe from a regimental striped pouch. He took a chair opposite Quist's desk. He got his pipe filled and lighted. Quist watched him, a faint smile at the corners of his mouth.

"Dan has told me what you're up to, Mr. Quist," Forrest

30

said. "May I say that your notion has a certain fascination for me."

Garvey was scowling. "George has met Trail," he said. "He spent an hour in conference with him."

"Why aren't you happy, Daniel?" Quist asked.

"Because your screwy idea has started George having screwy ideas," Garvey said.

Forrest smiled, and his smile made him look younger. He puffed contentedly on his pipe. "You probably know," he said, "that I handled an antitrust suit against the Trail Interests for the Attorney General two years ago."

Quist nodded.

"I lost the case," Forrest said. "To protect my own vanity, Mr. Quist, I was the trial lawyer. The Attorney General's office prepared the case. I think I was very good at the trial; my cross-examination was first-rate. We lost the case because several key witnesses either disappeared or refused to testify when the time came. I began to understand then the real power of Trail Interests. But that isn't what interests you, is it? There was an occasion before the case went to trial when there was a conference between Trail's lawyers and the prosecution. I represented the Attorney General, along with a couple of assistants. We proposed to reduce the severity of the indictment if Trail would plead guilty to a lesser charge."

"And Trail was present," Garvey said.

Forrest smiled at Quist. "I think," he said.

Quist's eyes narrowed. "You *think?*"

"The meeting was held in the plush conference room of the Shannon Oil Company on Wall Street. Trail owns Shannon Oil. There were a half dozen of the top corporation lawyers in the country representing Trail. At the head of the table was a man who was introduced to me as Trail."

"You're teasing me, Forrest," Quist said.

"At the time I was surprised," Forrest said. "The man introduced to me as Trail was conservatively dressed, and he wore large black glasses that hid all facial expression. In the course of an hour he never spoke a word. He nodded 'yes' or 'no' to questions from us or from his lawyers. If a more elaborate answer was required, he would gesture toward one of his lawyers who would promptly supply the answer. When we finally reached an impasse he simply stood up and left the room. If I'd met him on the street a day later without the glasses, I don't think I could have identified him."

"Sounds like a carefully planned act by a big-shot mystery man," Quist said. "Was it the act that surprised you?"

"No," Forrest said. He tamped down the tobacco in his pipe and puffed at it. "We had done very thorough research on Trail and his Empire," he said. "There is almost no information on Trail, where he was born, educated. Dan tells me you discovered that blank in *Who's Who*. But the history of Trail Interests goes back a long way—twenty-five, thirty years. Trail, I assumed, would have to be in his late fifties, perhaps early sixties."

"So you didn't hear him speak, you didn't really have a good look at his face," Quist said.

"Hands," Forrest said. "Hands have always fascinated me, Mr. Quist. I watch a witness on the stand, and I watch his hands. They tell you a lot; how nervous he is, how hard he is trying to control his feelings; how well he takes care of himself physically. Chewed fingernails tell a story. But hands tell you something else, Mr. Quist. A man's hands reveal his age."

"So?"

"The man introduced to me as Jeremy Trail was no more than in his mid-thirties."

"You think they pulled a ringer on you?" Quist asked.

"Would you believe that didn't occur to me at the time?" Forrest said. "Let me tell you how it was. When this man appeared in the conference room and took his place at the head of the table he was introduced as 'Mr. Trail.' Take note of that, Mr. Quist. He was not introduced as 'Mr. Jeremy Trail'; just 'Mr. Trail.' I had never heard of any other Mr. Trail, so I assumed, of course, that he was Jeremy Trail. Until I'd studied his hands for a while."

"So he was a ringer."

"I came to quite another conclusion," Forrest said. "This man, at that conference, had to make certain key decisions. He made them—with a nod or a gesture. He couldn't have been schooled in advance. Now, understand, Trail didn't *have* to attend that meeting. His lawyers could have handled it for him. He chose to come. There was no reason to fake his presence. Afterwards—after I'd fretted about his hands—I decided that the 'Mr. Trail' who'd been at that meeting was either Jeremy Trail's son, or a younger brother, or a cousin. He was there because Jeremy Trail needed someone present he could trust beyond any doubt. Our man was only what you call a ringer in the sense that we were allowed to assume that he was Jeremy Trail when actually he was some other Trail."

Quist toyed with one of his long, thin cigars without lighting it. "What would happen to the Empire if Jeremy Trail were to die?" he asked.

Forrest frowned. "Trail is the King of that Empire," he said. "When he dies there will be a dozen other big shots scrambling for power. It would be felt in the stock market. The Empire could begin to crumble."

"A lot of people would lose a lot of money?"

"A great deal of money."

Quist finally took the time to light his cigar. "So it would be worth someone's time," he said, watching the smoke curl upward, "to keep Trail alive after he was dead."

Forrest considered this for a moment. "His wife, his children if there are any, someone personally close to him. Trail is the superpower of the Empire. Without him there'd be, as

33

I've said, a dozen powerhouses trying to grab the top spot."

"His wife talks about him as very much alive, sexually vigorous," Quist said.

"You want a guess from me, don't you, Mr. Quist?"

"I really don't want a guess, Forrest. I want facts."

"The best I can do is guess. It's my guess that the man I met as 'Mr. Trail' was not Jeremy Trail. That was two years ago, remember. I'm guessing that Jeremy Trail couldn't be there and had a relative sit in for him, so that he'd have an unimpeachable report of what went on. My guess is that Jeremy Trail is not dead. It couldn't have been kept a secret for very long. He could be ill, but still hanging onto his power through a stand-in."

"And he could never have existed at all," Quist said. "He could have been invented by two or three of those power-houses you've mentioned as a front for their control of Trail Interests."

"I doubt that," Forrest said. Then he shook his head. "Yet the complete lack of any personal history: place of birth, parents, schooling—"

"An interesting blank," Quist said. "The suit that the Government brought against Trail was an antitrust action. The same kind of action has been brought against some of the bluest-chip companies in the nation, Forrest. It's a violation of the law, it's in restraint of trade, free competition, what have you. But we tend not to think of it as crime like murder, or kidnapping, or drug peddling—like the activities of what we call the Syndicate, or the Mafia. Right?"

"Right."

"So, during your investigation of Trail Interests did you ever come across evidence or rumors of criminal activity in the sense I mean?"

Forrest nodded. "But nothing provable," he said. "There are always rumors where there is power. There have been rumors of a traffic in drugs, but no Government agencies

34

have come up with a shred of evidence to back them up. They are rumored to have supported the Arab cause in the Middle East with money and munitions. They do own oil supplies in that part of the world. But so far as I know the C.I.A. has never come up with anything. They are said to control illegal gambling setups, which could involve illegal traffic in women, the murder of opposition factions. There could be a kind of superblackmail: using their power and influence to force less powerful groups to play the game their way." Forrest looked directly at Quist. "Dan thinks they might put you out of business if you persist in this guessing game. They could, you know, without your being able to prove they know you exist."

"But you think these rumors of crime are just pipe dreams of people who hate Trail Interests for one reason or another, or just like to invent sensations?"

"I didn't say I didn't believe them," Forrest said. "I said they hadn't been proved."

Quist smiled. "You are about as direct as a corkscrew, my friend," he said.

"You're talking about a corkscrew kind of world, Mr. Quist. Let me tell you what I think I think." Forrest chuckled and paused to knock out his pipe. "That *is* a kind of corkscrew statement, isn't it—'what I think I think'? I had drawn certain conclusions about Trail Interests which have been slightly upset by Dan's report to me about your Colonel Brownlow. Is there no one who knows Trail personally, intimately? Except his wife, who could be part of a setup? Before I got tickled by that suggestion, Mr. Quist, I had decided about my 'Mr. Trail' as follows: There certainly was a Jeremy Trail, despite the absence of a known background. The Empire couldn't have been put together by a phantom. He existed and I think he exists. He can't be everywhere in the world at the same time, so someone, or perhaps more than one person, stands in for him from time to time.

There's a second possibility, and as we've talked I find myself wondering if it may not be true."

"I am all ears," Quist said.

"My second thought is that 'Jeremy Trail' is a name and not a person at all. I mean by that, someone uses 'Jeremy Trail' as a trade name. That someone, let us say, is well-known 'John Smith.' Smith is no phantom, but 'Jeremy Trail' is, you might say, his stage name. When you and I want an answer to a direct question they don't want to answer, we are referred to the unreachable 'Jeremy Trail.' All the time John Smith, who is the real power, is standing at our elbow. Someone is real, Mr. Quist. Someone is the one-man king of the Empire. He is either a real Jeremy Trail, or someone who has used that name for years as a nom de plume."

"And the truth would be fascinating," Quist said, softly.

"It's not a parlor game!" Garvey said.

"My dear Daniel," Quist said, "you know that I can't bear unsolved puzzles." He leaned forward to put his cigar in the ash tray on his desk. "I am going to undertake Colonel Brownlow's request to promote the *Queen Alexandria* as a nautical museum. Tomorrow Lydia and I will go out with him on the pilot boat to meet the *Queen*. Hopefully we'll make contact with Mrs. Trail's party. What we do from there on in depends on the feel of things." He grinned. "Frankly, I can't wait to meet the most beautiful woman in the world."

"And get your brains bashed in!" Garvey said.

Lydia Morton had an apartment of her own just a block and a half away from Quist's Beekman Place establishment. Arrangements had been made for Quist to pick her up at a few minutes after nine to proceed to a North River pier where the pilot boat was to make a special stop to take them aboard along with Colonel Brownlow. With her

36

breakfast coffee Lydia read Myra Rudolph's column. Myra had not waited to spring her little surprise.

Today everyone who is anyone will attend a wingding given on board the *Queen Alexandria* at Pier Ninety-one as a sort of farewell to that great old ship which will have completed her last voyage as a luxury liner. . . . This reporter can hardly wait to contact an old friend, the glamorous Sophia Trail who is making the final trip on the *Alexandria*. We mean to ask Sophia if there is any basis to the current rumor that her husband doesn't exist and, if that should be true, who it is who helps her to keep looking so gloriously happy. . . .

Mrs. Trail would not be happy with that little item, Lydia thought. It was all that was needed to start a thousand tongues wagging.

Lydia had chosen to wear a white sharkskin pantsuit for the excursion. She had a dizzying picture of herself climbing some sort of rope ladder to board the *Alexandria* with Colonel Brownlow peering up at her from the deck of the pilot boat. A skirt, she had decided, was not ideal for such a moment. She wore a raspberry-colored blouse under her suit jacket with earrings and a straw handbag to match.

Her doorbell rang a few minutes after nine and she went downstairs to join Quist. He was standing beside a taxi, resplendent in a navy blue slacks, a navy blue turtleneck knitted shirt, and a white linen jacket. His blond hair looked almost like a golden wig in the sunlight.

In the back of the cab her hand reached out for his. "Did you see Myra's column?" she asked.

He nodded, frowning.

"Just what do you expect of me, Julian?"

He looked down at her, the frown gone. "I expect you to be very obviously with me, love," he said. "I don't want

37

Mrs. Trail writing me down as another lone wolf out to have her for lunch. You look delicious, by the way."

"Thank you, sir. I missed you last night."

"I, too." He was frowning again. "I don't know just how this is going to play, Lydia. Maybe Myra has given us the wedge we need. I can joke about the 'rumor' without seeming to have invented it myself. I want to know who travels with Madam; who seems to be close to her. There must be someone close to her who also knows Trail—if he exists. Madam obviously plays her role expertly; there may be someone else in the party whose foot might slip. I'll value your judgment, Lydia."

"I have the feeling that no one in the Trail camp makes mistakes, Julian."

"The mistake could be so small, darling," Quist said. "A frown when a smile is called for; a turn of the head that betrays surprise or anger. Keep your eyes peeled. I'll be concentrating on the Madam."

"Lucky her!"

He leaned toward her and kissed a little ringlet of dark hair at her temple. "Don't turn green," he said. "It won't go with that raspberry shirt."

Colonel Brownlow looked very jaunty when they met him at the pier. He had on gray flannel slacks, a dark blue blazer with a Players Club patch at the breast pocket, and a Panama hat worn at a rakish angle. He eyed Lydia with a connoisseur's relish when they were introduced.

"I hope you don't object to a gal in trousers, Colonel," Lydia said. "I had a vision of myself climbing a rope ladder."

"Lord, no," the Colonel said. "There's a door in the hull of the ship that opens up. You just step off the bridge of the pilot boat into the *Queen*. No problem except in rough weather. Today the ocean is glass-smooth."

38

The pilot boat, about the size of an ocean-going tug but with much more brass and polish, was waiting at the pier. The three passengers were conducted to deck chairs just outside the wheelhouse.

"If the sun's too much for you, ma'am," the boat's mate said to Lydia, "the Captain will be happy to make his cabin available."

"Out here is fine," Lydia said.

The boat's engines rumbled under their feet and they moved out into the North River and down the harbor, the great gray-green figure of the Statue of Liberty off to their left.

The Colonel seemed to be in the grip of an unusual excitement. "You saw Myra Rudolph's column?" he asked Quist. "What does that do to us?"

"Helps, I think," Quist said. "Helps us ask the questions without seeming to be the initiators."

The Colonel took a folded slip of paper from his inside pocket. "I managed to get a copy of the passenger list from the Whitehall Company," he said. "Mrs. Trail's in A Seventy-seven, one of the most luxurious cabins on the *Queen*. Paneled in weathered sycamore wood. It's a double, of course, but she's in it alone. Air conditioning, the works. General Marshall had it on one of my trips."

"She would have the best," Quist said.

"I've picked out five other names that may be of use to you," the Colonel said. "There is a Margaret Thompson in a single on A deck. She's a sort of paid companion and secretary to Sophia Trail. Handles all the lady's social engagements. I've met her. Very cool type. She says all the 'no's,' so that Mrs. Trail can always say the charming 'yes's.' Margaret Thompson will always have her eye on you."

"The others on your list?" Quist asked.

"All on A deck," the Colonel said. "There's Benjamin Clyde, who is said to be Trail's personal lawyer. There's

39

Horace Van Dine, who is president of the Trail Shipping Interests. Those two will be key figures in trying to make a deal for the *Queen*. Then there is one Anthony Cremona— Tony Cremona. He's a dark, Italian fellow, rumored to be some sort of distant relative of Mrs. Trail's. She was a Pravelli, you know. Friend of mine in Interpol swears Cremona is in the drug racket, but they've never been able to nail him. He's high up in the Trail empire. Mystery man."

"And number five?"

"Saved the most interesting till last," the Colonel said. "His name is Neil Patrick. The lady never goes anywhere without him. Handsome as a movie star. Drives high-powered racing cars, sails boats, dances like a professional, gambles. Always wins—suspiciously always. Good poker players tell me he's the best they've ever encountered. There've been whispers that he isn't above a little bottom dealing, but no one's caught him out. In my judgment he is purely and simply the lady's bodyguard." The Colonel glanced at Lydia. "He may be other things to her, but his job is 'guard the treasure.' You look at him, Quist, you'll find he's always smiling, always gay, but has the cold eyes of a killer. My advice, always keep him in front of you where you can see him."

Quist's eyes were narrowed against the bright sunlight. Lydia had produced a pair of black glasses from her straw handbag. They were out of the mouth of the harbor now, heading toward their meeting with the *Queen*.

"Could Neil Patrick be Jeremy Trail?" Quist asked.

"Lord, no," the Colonel said, indulging in an explosive little laugh. "His background is well known. British. Father was a wine merchant, mother a third-rate actress. Neil Patrick was kicked out of at least three good schools. Got into Oxford somehow, and out somehow before he could graduate. Tried the theatre without success, except with the ladies. Got to racing cars. Was good at it. Got himself invited to Trail's island a few years back—and never left. Neil Patrick is Neil Patrick, no one else." The Colonel stood up abruptly. "There she is, by God!"

On the horizon they saw the giant, three-funneled *Queen Alexandria*.

CHAPTER FIVE

She seemed unbelievable to Lydia as the pilot boat eased alongside. "Longer than three football fields," the Colonel told her. The great ship's hull was black, with white superstructure, and three red funnels, tipped with black. Hundreds of people leaned over the rails of the various decks, watching the pilot boat come alongside.

A door opened in the hull and a short gangway was hooked to the bridge rail of the pilot boat. Two sailors reached out to help Lydia aboard. She and the Colonel and Quist were whisked up in an elevator to the top deck. A deck officer accompanied them to the Captain's cabin where the Colonel and his guests were expected.

The Captain's sitting room was furnished with comfortable overstuffed chairs and a couch. A stretcher table in the center of the room was loaded down with drink makings and silver platters of hors d'oeuvres. Captain Ligget was greeting the pilot, and a young staff officer acted as host.

"Captain Ligget hopes you will wait till he can join you, Colonel," the officer said. "The party's already started in the main dining room. All very bright and gay. Not easy for us to get into the spirit of it, I'm afraid."

"Doesn't seem possible," the Colonel said. "Last time she'll put into port. Like killing a friend who's in perfect health."

"We've heard rumors, sir, that you may keep her intact."

"Pray for me," the Colonel said. "Mr. Quist and Miss Morton are going to try to help me."

"We'll pray for all of you," the officer said. "From what I've heard you may need it. The Trail people seem quite confident she'll belong to them."

Quist was pouring Scotch on the rocks for himself and Lydia. "How do they show their confidence?" he asked.

"Horace Van Dine has had cocktails here with the Captain," the officer said. "He's head of Trail Shipping, you know. He suggested to Captain Ligget that he leave the Whitehall Company and command the *Alexandria* for Trail. There seemed to be no doubt in his mind that Trail would be the new owner."

"The game isn't over yet," the Colonel muttered.

"How did the Captain react?" Quist asked.

"Not with favor, sir," a strong voice said from the doorway. Captain Ligget was a handsome, gray-haired man in his late fifties, his strong, weatherbeaten face set in a grim smile. "Hello, Colonel. Delightful to see you again. Wish the circumstances were happier."

"All things come to an end, Richard," the Colonel said. "You get to accept that at my age." He introduced Lydia and Quist. "Mr. Quist is a public relations expert, Richard. He's going to try to help me keep the *Queen* out of Trail's hands."

"I wish I believed you could be successful, sir," the Captain said.

Quist sipped his Scotch. "Trail apparently plans to keep the *Queen* afloat, Captain, not break her up for scrap. Why does that displease you?"

"You might not understand, Mr. Quist," Ligget said. "I

43

was a staff captain on the *Queen* in the Colonel's time. She has a history of heroism and honor. She served her country and her country's allies. If she is to be buried, she should be buried with honor, not turned into a playground for gamblers and criminals. I would rather die than see her wind up her career under a flag of shame. I have resented having to carry her would-be destroyers on this last voyage."

"What makes you think Trail represents gamblers and criminals, Captain?" Quist asked.

The Captain's face turned expressionless. "It's probably idle gossip," he said. "But—but you hear a great deal of talk in a job like mine. One thing I do know, Mr. Quist. I shouldn't care to cross swords with Trail, no matter how skillful I was. To alter an old saying to fit the facts, you might win the battle but you could never win the war." Ligget straightened his shoulders. "I regret to say that I must join the festivities in the main dining room. Please feel free to stay here as long as you like. It will be some two hours before we dock."

"You could do me a favor, Captain, that might help the Colonel's chances," Quist said. "I take it you know Mrs. Trail?"

"Of course. She sat at my table during this crossing—at my right."

"Fine. When we come downstairs to the party I'd like you to find an opportunity to introduce me to her. I'd like not to seem to pick her up if it can be avoided."

Ligget gave him a tight smile. "You couldn't pick her up if you tried, Mr. Quist. Not with Neil Patrick at her side. Yes, I can manage an introduction."

"It would be just as well not to mention that I'm a friend of Colonel Brownlow's."

Ligget shook his head. "If it matters to her she already knows," he said. "I was standing a few yards away from her

44

while she watched your party come aboard from the pilot boat."

"Well, thanks for preventing me from putting my foot into that one," Quist said.

The main dining room of the *Queen Alexandria* left Lydia a little breathless. She had been in most of the great hotels in America and London and Paris, but she'd never seen anything to match the elegance and richness of this room. Colonel Brownlow, at her elbow, was a bit like a tour guide. He was explaining to her that all the first-class passengers could be fed at one sitting in this magnificent room. The high ceiling was supported by fluted Grecian columns. The lighting was indirect and expert. There were beautifully painted murals depicting nineteenth century scenes of English life. Under normal circumstances it must have been a place of serene quiet, with a small string orchestra playing on the bandstand at the far end.

Now it was a madhouse.

It was only a little after noon, but more than a thousand people were already high and celebrating. Some of them had tried sitting at the tables but there was danger of being trampled to death. The ship's dance band was at work, and a clarinet screamed in competition with hundreds of shrieking women. Lydia thought she had never seen so many expensive clothes and so much fabulous jewelry under one roof. She felt a gentle pressure on her left arm and looked up at Quist. He nodded toward a near corner of the room.

A young woman was holding court there, and Lydia didn't have to be told that this was Sophia Trail. Lydia had long since made a perfectly unemotional evaluation of her own looks. She was aware that when she walked down Fifty Avenue on a shopping tour men turned to look at her. She enjoyed the compliment. She felt, without vanity, that she walked in no woman's shadow. But Sophia Trail was something else!

It was a subtle "something else." Her clothes weren't mod or far out, but Lydia's knowledgeable eye told her that Sophia's kind of simplicity had cost a fortune. But it wasn't her clothes. She had an exquisite figure, nowhere overemphasized, but it wasn't her figure. She had a handsome, high-cheekboned face and a wide, generous mouth, but it wasn't her face. Her eyes were wide; at a distance Lydia couldn't tell whether they were a dark blue or black. But it wasn't her eyes. All those things together added up to a woman of great natural beauty, but there was more than that. Just looking at her she had a kind of electric excitement that Lydia didn't remember seeing in anyone before. She felt pale and washed out by comparison. She looked up, almost apprehensively, at Quist. Somehow she didn't want him to be looking at Sophia Trail.

He was looking, his eyes slightly narrowed. "Quite a dish," he said. He turned, searching for Captain Ligget.

Lydia found herself irresistibly drawn back to Sophia Trail. There was a tall man standing beside her, and Sophia's white gloved hand rested casually on his arm. The man, too, was "something else." From what the Colonel had said this had to be Neil Patrick. He looked like a young Cary Grant. There was a kind of elegant theatricality about even his small movements. Always smiling, always gay the Colonel had said. He was too far away for Lydia to recognize what the Colonel had called "killer's eyes," but not too far for her to be unaware of an enormous physical excitement. She felt ashamed of noticing it, of reacting to it. She felt certain that these two extraordinarily glamorous people, Sophia Trail and Neil Patrick, could not be together all the time, as the Colonel had suggested, and stay casual.

There was amusement in Quist's voice. "Your mouth is open, love," he said. "Mr. Patrick *is* quite a hunk of man.

Brace yourself. Here comes Ligget. You're about to get a close-up."

Close up, Lydia found, it was worse. She felt like a shy, awkward schoolgirl. She was aware, when Captain Ligget introduced them, that Sophia Trail gave her a quick, appraising look and wrote her off.

"You are the enemy, Mr. Quist," Sophia said, turning her attention to something that interested her more than Lydia. She had a low, husky, disturbing voice with the faintest of accents.

"Enemy?" Quist said.

"You came aboard with Colonel Brownlow, and the poor old Colonel is the enemy."

Quist was not easily taken off balance, but Lydia realized he hadn't been prepared for the direct attack. Sophia was laughing at him.

"If he is your enemy he is mine," Quist said. "But why should he be your enemy?"

"I had a whim, Mr. Quist. I decided I wanted this lovely ship for my very own. My husband calls it a whim of iron. I mean to have her. The Colonel is a small obstacle in the way, but almost too small to notice."

Neil Patrick's eyes were gray, Lydia saw, and they were fixed on her. She felt as if she was being undressed in public in the middle of the *Queen Alexandria*'s dining room. Her hands felt cold. She found herself reaching out for Quist as though she needed his protection. But Quist was involved in a counterthrust.

"From what I read in Myra Rudolph's column this morning I was wondering how real your husband is, Mrs. Trail."

Sophia laughed. "Myra is a naughty girl," she said.

And in that moment Lydia saw the "killer eyes." For just an instant she saw cold anger in the eyes that had been caressing her; Patrick's smile seemed to freeze. And then he was himself again. Maybe that was the small thing Quist

47

had wanted her to watch for.

A waiter came, passing a tray of champagne. The moment passed.

"Are you some sort of reporter, Miss Morton?" Patrick asked, pleasantly British-sounding.

"What on earth makes you think so?" she asked.

"Coming out on the pilot boat," he said. "Are you here to find out if there is any truth to Myra's rumor?"

Lydia fought to sound casual. "No such thing," she said, "though, of course, I'm wildly curious. But my boss is a friend of Colonel Brownlow's. He invited us to be his guests at this final binge on the *Queen*."

"You work for Quist?"

"Yes."

"You could never work for me, Miss Morton."

"Oh?"

"You're far too disturbing."

"Thanks, I needed that," Lydia said. "It's not easy to stand here beside Mrs. Trail."

"Don't worry about her, Miss Morton," Patrick said. "She's far too involved with her husband to be a threat to you."

"So Myra's wrong, there is a husband?"

Patrick's laugh was attractive. "The husband of all time," he said. "If you meet him sometime you'll understand why we mere mortals are no threat to him."

"Does he never come to America?"

Patrick laughed again. "He's never public about anything he does."

"Then how does a mere mortal get to meet him?"

For just a flicker the cold look came back into Patrick's eyes. "Cross him," he said.

The brief exchange ended there. With a threat, Lydia thought. A party of four people bore down on Sophia. They had been fellow passengers on the trip. They were already stoned. Sophia must join them with some other friends at the far end of the room. Quist and Lydia were ignored.

"We'll meet again, Mr. Quist, before the party's over," Sophia said, and allowed herself to be carried away.

Patrick gave Lydia a regretful little smile. "I hope I can count on seeing you again," he said, and went after Sophia. The palms of Lydia's hands felt damp.

"Nice going," Quist said. He was smiling down at her. "You heard?"

"Every word, my love."

"I feel as though I'd been raped!" Lydia said.

"Better than that," Quist said. "We've both been told to lay off. Cross Trail Interests and we can depend on being noticed. So maybe the Colonel has really put us onto something."

Lydia reached out for Quist's hands. "Let's drop it, Julian. These people are larger than life. They're not real! If they can buy this boat for a whim—! What Dan says is true. They could smash us into small bits."

"Your hands are cold," Quist said.

"Julian, I'm scared of them."

He smiled. "I'll tell you a secret, darling. She's not the most beautiful woman in the world."

Her mouth trembled. "Hold that thought," she said. "But, oh, Julian, let's go promote some nice clean politician or a movie star and forget about Jeremy Trail."

Before the *Alexandria* docked it seemed the party on board had no place to go, but when the people waiting on Pier Ninety-one swarmed aboard it reached a gigantic climax of human noise. Captain Ligget, watching the proceedings from a vantage point in the shopping center in the main square of the ship, expressed himself to Quist and Lydia with some bitterness.

"She has already been desecrated," he said. "People are

49

stealing everything that isn't nailed down for souvenirs—down to pots out of the galley!"

"What could Trail use this ship for, Captain?" Quist asked. "His wife says she just had the whim to have it for a toy. But seriously, there aren't too many places she can dock, are there?"

"Here, Southampton, Gourock in Scotland, Cherbourg, Sydney, two or three other places. She's not designed as a pleasure yacht, Mr. Quist. She has speed; the fastest thing afloat today. But she can't be hidden." The Captain shrugged. "The man's a king. I suspect he dreams of a floating palace." The Captain's face was grim. "There are no police on the high seas, Mr. Quist."

Lydia gave Quist a gentle nudge in the ribs. Almost running across the square toward the main entrance to the dining room was Myra Rudolph, wearing an absurd hat that looked like a bowl of fruit. Quist and Lydia moved after her.

Myra stood poised in the doorway, looking for someone. And then she spotted Sophia Trail and Neil Patrick and headed for them. The greeting was effusive. Myra embraced Sophia and kissed her. She stood on tiptoe and kissed Patrick. She looked around to make sure people had been watching. After a brief conversation Patrick took Myra's arm and led her away toward one of the bars at the far end of the room. A squat dark man, tanned almost African black, promptly joined Sophia. He wasn't quite as tall as she was. A gaudy diamond ring glittered on the little finger of his left hand.

"The Mafia type," Quist said. "Tony Cremona is my guess."

Cremona was scowling after Myra Rudolph and Patrick. Sophia was talking to him rapidly, probably in Italian, Lydia thought. The man nodded as he listened.

"So how do we catch up?" a woman's voice asked at Quist's elbow. It was his secretary, Miss Parmalee. She looked cool, organized, prepared for anything from larceny to lechery. With her was Bobby Hilliard, one of Quist's assistants. Bobby was modeled after a boyish Jimmy Stewart, tall, shy, awkward, conservative as to clothes, altogether charming in his own way. In the office he wore owlish horn-rimmed glasses, and he squinted around the crowded room now as though he needed them.

"You see the old gent in the blue blazer in the far corner?" Quist said. "That's my Colonel Brownlow. Get him to point out Benjamin Clyde, who's Trail's lawyer, and Horace Van Dine, who's president of Trail Shipping. Try to catch up with those two, ingratiate yourselves, and toss them Myra Rudolph's column. Is there really a Jeremy Trail? Let me know what happens."

"Would it be possible to indulge in a drink?" Miss Parmalee asked. "I feel like a foreigner without one."

"Without one you'd be immediately suspect," Quist said. He gave her a little slap on the rump. "Charge!" he said.

The last of the day's sun reflected in blood-red streaks on the surface of the East River. Quist, on his apartment terrace, stood by the rail looking down at an excursion boat tripping down stream, her decks crowded. He looked at the boat, but he didn't seem to see it.

Lydia sat in one of the wicker armchairs, watching him. A tiny frown marred her lovely forehead. Inside the apartment Bobby Hilliard was puttering at the bar. Connie Parmalee came out of the john. She looked a little ruffled. Some of her cool was gone.

"Scotch?" Hilliard asked.

"I'll have a double Alka Seltzer," the girl said. "I never drank so much champagne in my life." She went on out to the terrace and sat down facing Lydia. "Maybe it was worth it," she said. "I have the offer of three different bed companions for tonight."

Hilliard, who had followed her out carrying a drink, laughed. "Four, Connie. Don't forget I'm always on the waiting list, right behind Garvey. That adds up to five, doesn't it?"

The granny glasses turned his way. "Let me know when you're serious," she said. She shook her head. "Damndest people I ever met."

Quist turned from the railing. "The Trail group?"

Connie nodded. "You gave me two names, boss," she said. "Benjamin Clyde, Trail's lawyer, and Horace Van Dine, head of the shipping interests. I expected two old gents, the kind you might see sitting in the window of a London club. Did you spot them?"

"No."

"Sun tan," Connie said, "produced by a special golden sun. I'd guess they're each about fifty, but these men jog or something. Never saw two men their age in such shape. Physical, physical, physical. Eyes so bright, as though they used belladonna drops to keep them that way. Strong white teeth that smile and smile. And charm; manners right out of a glittering drawing-room comedy. And sex, my friend. You can feel it like a charge when you're standing six feet away from them. They don't ask you, you understand, but you know they're suggesting it and—and I'm damned if you don't feel inclined to say yes. They're like people from another planet. There must be some kind of elixir of youth on that island of Trail's." She looked at Lydia. "You got the treatment from Patrick, didn't you?"

"I know what you mean," Lydia said. "A curious kind of built-in excitement."

"If you can control your libido for a moment, Connie," Quist said, "What happened when you asked the gentlemen about Myra's rumor?"

"Oh yes, I remembered to drop that little bomb," Connie said. "Mr. Clyde, who has a distinguished sprinkling of gray

52

at his temples that you know must be premature, thought the suggestion was hilariously funny. If I would care to visit his apartment, he has a raft of snapshots of Jeremy Trail."

"That would seem to make your choice of a bed companion easy."

Connie shuddered slightly. "Fortunately for me Mr. Clyde's apartment is in London. If I'd care to hop over there with him tomorrow or the next day—"

"And Van Dine?"

"Just as amused," Connie said. "And the next time Trail is in town he'd be glad to introduce me. Meanwhile—" She shrugged.

"Was Neil Patrick your third possible?" Quist asked.

"No such luck. Or maybe it was lucky, because I think I'd have said 'yes' to him and damn the torpedoes. No, my third suitor was the Mafia—Tony Cremona. He's short, built like an ape, no polish, but physical! When I asked him about Myra's rumor he said she ought to have her behind kicked —only he didn't say 'behind.' Then he asked if I liked Italian food, and if I did there was a very special place he'd like to take me for dinner tonight. And after dinner—" Connie closed her eyes. "I think I hope that in the future you'll limit my job for Quist Associates to taking your dictation and answering your phone. Or maybe I don't, but the next time I might not come back!"

"Nothing from your gentlemen to suggest anger or concern?"

"Nothing, except Cremona's suggestion of what should be done to Myra's posterior. I think, boss, they were prepared for us. The snow job they had waiting for a helpless office worker was brilliantly prepared."

Quist looked at Hilliard. "You, Bobby?"

"I agree with Connie," Hilliard said. "They were ready. My moment was with Miss Margaret Thompson, Sophia Trail's companion-secretary. And let me tell you, Julian, she found me, not the other way around. Maggie to her friends, is Miss Thompson. No more than thirty, I'd guess. Joan Crawford at that age; wide mouth, big eyes, cool—oh so cool. Behind that cool exterior is Woman with a capital W. Same kind of charge Connie is talking about in the men. I felt like a silly schoolboy with her."

"I know the feeling," Lydia said.

Quist smiled. "Did she offer to show you her etchings, Bobby?"

"Lord, no. I'm not nearly sophisticated enough to be her dish. She explained to me, like someone telling a small child the facts of life, that Trail is very real. When they are on the island she sees him every day of her life. Myra's suggestion, she assured me, is totally absurd. Then she, figuratively, patted my cheek and told me to run along back to my toys."

The doorbell rang.

"Must be Dan," Quist said. "Do you mind, Bobby?"

Hilliard went to the door and opened it to Garvey, a dark, angry-looking Garvey. He joined the others on the terrace. His eyes were two burning coals.

"You people haven't been listening to the radio or TV?" he asked.

"God forbid," Quist said. "What's eating you, Daniel?"

"A little less than an hour ago they fished a body out of the North River a couple of piers down from the *Queen Alexandria*'s berth," Garvey said. "Head smashed in, maybe from a fall. The blow on the head killed her. She didn't drown."

"Her?" Quist said.

"Myra Rudolph," Garvey said.

"Oh my God!" It was a whisper from Lydia.

"Let's not kid ourselves it was an accident," Garvey said, his voice harsh. "So will you quit now, Julian? You got Myra into that. Which one of us do you think may be next?"

Part 2

The little excursion boat tooted cheerfully at an oil tanker plodding up the river. Quist, his back to that scene, stared at Garvey, his pale blue eyes turned glacial.

"Details," he said.

"Not much yet," Garvey said. He looked at Hilliard. "Make me a Jack Daniels on the rocks, will you, Bobby? God how I hate this business; have hated it from the start. You're meddling with a meat chopper, Julian."

"Details," Quist said.

"There's a cruise ship, the *Santa Louisa,* berthed at Pier Eighty-nine," Garvey said. "Only crew aboard. She doesn't sail for several days; loading stores, other stuff. One of the crew was swabbing the deck near the stern when he saw a body bumping against the pilings. He got help and they fished it out and called the river police. There was no trouble makng an identification. Myra was carrying one of those shoulder-strap hand bags. It stayed with her. Driver's license, credit cards, all that."

"Oh God!" Lydia whispered.

"How did you hear?" Quist asked.

"I was in John Riley's office when the word came in. I

thought Riley might have an answer to the Trail mystery if there was one."

John Riley was Manhattan's district attorney. Riley had made a run for the United States Senate back in '68 and Julian Quist Associates had handled his public relations campaign. Riley had lost in the primaries, but he'd remained cordial and friendly with Dan Garvey, who had been his direct contact with the Quist office.

"Riley thinks it's murder?" Quist asked.

Garvey shrugged. He took a swallow of the drink Hilliard brought him. "He'd read Myra's column this morning. We'd just been talking about Trail when the word came. Two and two could, sometimes, add up to four. There were a lot of drunken people on the Alexandria. She might have fallen overboard, but how do you fall overboard surrounded by fifteen hundred people without being seen? Myra Rudolph wouldn't wander off from a party like that. She'd be in the middle of the action. That's her job."

"If she got herself a little overstoned?" Hilliard suggested.

"Not Myra," Lydia said. "She handles—handled—her liquor very carefully. When other people are high that's when Myra gets her best gossip. Oh, God, Julian, I did give her the idea. If it hadn't been for me—"

"Stop it," Quist said, sharply. He took one of his thin cigars out of his breast pocket and turned it round and round in his fingers. "Before what you call 'the word' came to Riley, did he have any opinion about Trail's existence?"

"Same old story," Garvey said. "Doesn't know anyone who has actually said he knows Trail. You take it for granted that people like his lawyer Benjamin Clyde, and Horace Van Dine and Felix Hargrove, his own men, know him. And his wife, of course. You have no reason *not* to think he's real."

"Until the question comes up," Quist said.

"Right." Garvey finished his drink in two gulps and

handed his glass to Hilliard for a refill. "Let's face it, Julian. The whole damned world is a spider web with Trail, real or unreal, in the center of it: a man-eating spider waiting for the unsuspected fly to crawl in. A fly like Myra, or you, or me, or Lydia, or any of us. They don't want your question answered, Julian."

"They don't know we're involved," Quist said.

"Of course they know," Garvey said. "You can bet that half an hour after I asked Felix Hargrove my question he knew who I was, who I worked for. Your stupid old bastard of a colonel talks too much. He told his friend in the Players, didn't he? They've already connected you with the Colonel. You came aboard the *Alexandria* with him. It's ten-to-one that somebody knows that Lydia had cocktails with Myra yesterday, and the next morning the question is in Myra's column. They know, Julian. They know about us."

"How do we back out—if we want to?" Connie Parmalee asked. She looked as if she was just recovering from accident shock.

"How do you back out of a landslide?" Garvey said. "We can go to them, hat and hand, and promise to be good children; say we're not really interested. Will they risk believing us?" His laugh was bitter. "So I get run down by a taxi. It's an accident, just like Myra's. So Lydia falls in front of a subway train. Tragic. So Julian is mugged and killed by some alleged hophead, out to get some bread for a fix. That's how it will be, friends."

Quist lit his cigar. "So we have no choice," he said, quietly. "We have to hit them before they hit us."

"Julian!" It was a little cry from Lydia.

"The truth about Trail is how we stay in one piece," Quist said. "We've been going about it casually. Now we have to charge—or else."

"I believe it was Stephen Leacock who described a hero as 'riding off in all directions at once,'" Connie Parmalee said. She was her cool, organized self again. "Charge where, boss?"

"Whatever the truth is about Trail it will clearly endanger the Empire," Quist said. "He'd dead; he never existed; he is sick, has become a vegetable."

"Suppose they fail to stop us and we discover the truth," Garvey said. "Then there is a little matter of revenge."

Quist's smile was thin. "They just might be too busy picking up the pieces to bother with us any longer," he said. "We can't just sit here, children, waiting for somebody to lower the boom on us."

There were several police cars at the mouth of Pier Ninety. The *Queen Alexandria* was strangely quiet after the bedlam of the party. In the darkness her black hull loomed high above Quist's head. A uniformed cop was standing at the foot of a short gangway opening into the side of the ship.

"My name is Julian Quist."

The cop nodded. "Lieutenant Kreevich is expecting you. He's set up in the Captain's cabin. If you go aboard and take the automatic elevator just to the left of—"

"I know where the cabin is," Quist said.

Dan Garvey had contacted the District Attorney and arranged for Quist to talk to the Homicide man who was investigating Myra Rudolph's death. Lieutenant Kreevich was a short, square man who seemed to be concerned with making his boyish face look grim and tough.

The Captain's cabin was stripped of the party look. The liquor bottles and the canapés were gone. Kreevich was sitting at the table where they had been, a notebook in front of him. He was talking to one of the ship's crew. He nodded to Quist but went on with his interview.

"It's a bad thing to have happened," the sailor said, "because we were set up to prevent just that. The Captain had

had a watch on each deck. 'Some drunk is likely to fall overboard,' he told us."

"So all the open areas of the ship were patrolled?" Kreevich's voice was hoarse, aggressive.

"Looking for just this kind of thing to happen," the sailor said.

"And nobody saw this dame go over the side?"

"Positively not. We've checked out everyone. The party was pretty well concentrated in the dining room and the ship's square. There weren't many people on the decks, except on their way ashore. It would have been next to impossible for her to go over the side without being noticed."

"You didn't see her leave the ship?"

"Hell, Lieutenant, I don't even know what she looked like. There were close to two thousand people coming and going. All anyone was looking for was to keep people from going off with the light fixtures or the punch bowls. This was the biggest souvenir hunt in history."

"Anything else you can think of that might help?"

The sailor frowned. "We're tied up to the pier, Lieutenant. The starboard side of the ship is up tight against it. If she fell off that side she'd almost certainly have landed on the dock, not in the water. If she went off the port side you'd think the body would stay up against the ship, not two piers down. There's no current in the slip. It seems like she'd have to go off the stern end to float downstream. There's a wire barricade that keeps you from going right to the end of the ship. If she tried to climb over it, she'd be bound to have been noticed."

"So?"

"I figure she left the ship, walked down the pier, and fell off the other side of it."

"But none of your people saw her?"

"Hell, Lieutenant, we were concentrating on the ship, not the shore."

"Thanks," Kreevich said. "Will you tell the chief steward who was in charge in the dining room I'd like to see him in a few minutes."

The sailor gave Kreevich a casual salute and went out. Kreevich closed his eyes for a second, as if he was tuning to a new channel. "You're Julian Quist?"

"Yes."

Kreevich looked at Quist's bell-bottoms and his double-breasted blue jacket and his hair as if he didn't believe it.

"The D.A. gives you high marks for reliability, Mr. Quist," the detective said. "He seems to think you may be able to give us some help."

"I may be indirectly responsible for what happened to Miss Rudolph," Quist said.

Kreevich's dark eyebrows rose, but he didn't say anything. Quist put it on the line for him: Colonel Brownlow's suggestion that Trail was a myth; Lydia's passing the word along to Myra; the column, making the question public.

"And then, pow!" Kreevich said, scowling.

"Could be."

Kreevich scowled down at his notebook. "We have a preliminary report from the Medical Examiner," he said. "She didn't drown, which means she was dead when she hit the water. No water in the lungs. The back of her head was staved in. Flecks of metal and black paint in the wound." He looked up at Quist. "This is where we're incomplete at the moment. If she fell overboard and struck her head against the side of the ship, that could have produced metal and black paint. But she would have had to hit herself a hell of a belt. There are other things on the ship and on the pier that could leave a residue of metal flakes and black paint. I've seen a lot of wounds in my time, Mr. Quist. This wasn't a glancing blow, the kind you might expect if she struck her head in falling. It could have happened that way, but I'd be more inclined to think she was struck a savage blow with a piece of black painted pipe, maybe a belaying pin. The laboratory will tell us soon if it was the ship."

"Alcohol?" Quist asked.

"Almost no traces. She might have had a drink or two. Maybe at the party."

"Then she wasn't drunk?"

"Positively not."

"So the possibility of a drunken fall is out?"

"Entirely out—off the record. We're letting that supposition circulate, though. No point in alerting a possible killer that we're hunting him."

"So you think she was murdered?"

"No doubt of it in my mind," Kreevich said.

Quist's eyes narrowed. "If she was you can bet your next pay raise the Trail Interests are back of it."

Kreevich stared steadily at Quist. "My advice to you, Mr. Quist, is to back away from it. I can tell you in advance what is going to happen to me. I will be presented with some kind of a fall guy. For example, a dead sailor who will have, allegedly, tried to rape Miss Rudolph on a deserted pier, and killed himself out of remorse after he had killed her during her effort to resist him. There will be a convenient little note on the suicide, confessing all. Case closed."

"And if you don't buy it?"

"I'll be shifted to the burglary detail on Staten Island or in northern Westchester," Kreevich said.

"Are you telling me the Police Commissioner can be reached?" Quist asked.

"He doesn't have to be reached," Kreevich said, his voice bitter. "Some self-righteous little prick will show up who will say his conscience bothers him and reveal that I took a payoff from him to allow him to keep his bar open after closing hours, or to violate some building code or fire law. If he isn't believed, there will be other witnesses to support his charge. That's how the Trails of this world handle things."

"Then if I back off the case *will* be closed."

Kreevich brought the flat of his hand down on the table. "I can smell it," he said. "And if you don't back off, Mr. Quist, you are just a minnow in an ocean full of man-eating sharks."

The bar at The Players was relatively deserted. Two members sat at a round table, heads bent together in some private conversation. Two others were playing backgammon at one of the long tables, with a third member making derisive remarks about the caliber of play and taking doubles from one of the dice throwers.

Jack Worthington, the Colonel's little bald-headed chum, greeted Quist at the foot of the stairs leading down from the entryway.

"So how was the party?" Worthington asked. "I've been waiting for Brownlow to come back and tell me about it. He must have run into pals."

"The party was very gay," Quist said. "With the added spice of a murder, I should call it memorable."

"Murder!"

"Myra Rudolph."

"Somebody didn't like her column, eh? Come in, my dear fellow, and let me buy you a drink."

"A stirrup cup," Quist said. "I have places to go. I tried to reach the Colonel by phone earlier. I came by this way in the hope he'd have gotten back by now."

"No sign of him," Worthington said. "Good God! Murder! What'll it be?"

"It's been a champagne day," Quist said. "I think a brandy and soda, if I may."

"By all means." Worthington waved at the yellow-jacketed barman. "A brandy and soda for my guest, Juan, and a double Southern Comfort on the rocks for me." He took Quist's arm and pulled him down into a Windsor armchair at one of the tables. "Does Brownlow know?"

Quist shrugged. "If he's been near a TV set or a radio," he said.

"He wouldn't be caught dead near either if he could help it. How was it done?"

"Meant to look like a fall off the *Alexandria*. Question is, 'did she fall or was she pushed?' "

"And your guess?"

"Pushed—figuratively speaking," Quist said. "I thought Colonel Brownlow should be warned. I hope I'm wrong in thinking he may have talked too much about his theory— the Trail myth. Wonderful conversation piece for the cocktail hour or dinner. Somebody doesn't want it explored; wants the gossip stopped. Anyone who makes too much noise may wind up in an unpleasantness."

"Like getting killed?"

"Like getting killed, Mr. Worthington. The Colonel isn't totally unaware of danger. He once mentioned the possibility of our winding up on adjoining slabs in the morgue. I wanted him to know that we've been vividly reminded of that possibility. He should, in short, find some place to put his foot other than in his mouth."

"Well, yes!" Worthington said.

The drinks were delivered, and they raised their glasses in salute and drank.

"Care to give me any details about the Rudolph woman?" Worthington asked.

The brandy felt warm in Quist's stomach. He reminded himself to remember how much he really liked brandy. "Skull smashed in, found floating in the river," he said. "Not drowned. Killed by the blow to her head. That's all there is to know at the moment. The police are letting it be thought she may have joined a couple of thousand other people in getting drunk and toppled over the side. She wasn't drunk. Traces of alcohol at a real minimum. The police don't believe it was an accident, but they don't intend to say so at once."

"Why?"

"Because as soon as they say it's murder, we will be provided with a murderer—too dead to talk."

"Of course," Worthington said. "That's how they'd work it. Never let you get near the real killer."

Quist drank. "I hate to swallow this excellent brandy so quickly, Mr. Worthington, but there are others who need bringing up to date." He took his wallet out of his pocket and scribbled a number on a business card. He handed it to Worthington. "That is my unlisted home phone. Will you have the Colonel call me there when he gets in, no matter how late?"

A single shaded lamp was burning in Quist's living room when he let himself in. The orange glow from the fabric shade spread down on Lydia's shining dark hair. She was curled up in a corner of the couch, sound asleep.

The human nervous system, Quist thought, is a remarkable instrument. Let a beloved or someone familiarly a part of the household walk in on you while you're asleep and you remain oblivious. Let a stranger step on a squeaking floorboard thirty yards away and you are wide awake, alert. Lydia didn't move, nor did her gentle breathing alter its rhythm.

Quist looked down at her, his face relaxed. Then he sat down beside her on the edge of the couch. She was still wearing the white sharkskin pantsuit she'd chosen for the nonexistent rope-ladder climb onto the *Queen Alexandria*. He put his hand on her hip and ran it down the crisp material to the bend in her knee. Lydia made a sleepy, loving sound and opened her eyes.

"Hi," she said.

"I am against pantsuits," Quist said. "They deprive you of

the special pleasure of caressing a bare thigh."

"Lecher!" Lydia said. Then she sat up abruptly and reached out to him. "You're all right, Julian?"

"Sure I'm all right," Quist said. He stood up and wandered toward the bar. "Nightcap?"

"Must we?"

Quist reached down onto a lower shelf and produced a bottle of brandy. "I'm afraid, darling, this isn't a night for pleasure. Do I have to tell you how much I regret that?"

"Don't be foolish, Julian. When I'm not sure of how you feel I won't be napping on your couch. Can you tell me what's happening?"

Quist poured her a Scotch on the rocks and himself a brandy. He knew she hated brandy.

"I've been thinking of Jennifer Nyland, our Hollywood client," he said.

Lydia's eyes widened. "She turns you on?"

"Maybe," Quist said, studying the dark gold liquid in his glass. "I think perhaps we ought to really launch our campaign for her. I think you ought to take off for California in the morning and have a few days of heart-to-heart with our Jennifer."

"So you can have at Sophia Trail?" Lydia came across to the bar and picked up her drink. "Is it that bad, Julian?"

"My passion for Sophia?"

"Don't be an idiot, my darling. You think I may be in danger here."

"Could be." The casual effort didn't ring true.

"And you, Julian? There's danger for you?"

"There's danger in getting up in the morning," he said. "You slip on a piece of soap in your shower—"

"Level with me, darling," Lydia said.

He looked at her, directly. "Go to Hollywood. Set up Jennifer Nyland's campaign."

"No."

He gave her a crooked smile. "If you'd said anything else I'd have broken your arm. It's a bad business, love. I've been thinking about the either-ors ever since I left you. It's stay here with me and Dan to protect you, or it's disappear."

"Disappear?"

"We send you to Hollywood with a fanfare of trumpets and you disappear. I had Rex Roberts's little island in mind. You'd be hidden there." He smiled. "You might have to sleep with Rex to keep his cries of frustration from being heard on the mainland, but otherwise you'd be out of sight of Trail's mob."

Lydia sipped her Scotch. She looked over the rim of her glass, her eyes mischievous. "Rex might be fun at that," she said. "You're dead serious, aren't you, Julian?"

"Tonight I don't like the casual use of the word 'dead.'" Quist said. "In passing, Rex talks so much about his sexual prowess that you can be almost certain he isn't very good at it."

"So we've made our jokes," Lydia said. She reached across the bar and covered Quist's hand with hers. "How bad is it?"

His eyes narrowed. "It's like jungle fighting, my pet. You can't see the snipers for the trees. They know where you are, but you don't know where they are."

"So when you walk through the woods you wear camouflage."

"We've already been spotted," Quist said. He took a cigar out of a box on the bar and lit it. "Myra got just a half day of living out of a four-line item in her column. They didn't wait to see whether it started anything. They made sure she wouldn't carry on. Tomorrow may be our turn. There is a small thing in our favor, and perhaps we can enlarge on it. People of some importance know of our interest in the Trail myth: George Forrest, an attorney for the Justice Department; John Riley, the local D.A.; Lieutenant Kreevich of Homicide. They're not going to buy 'accident.' If we make a very big noise, plant the story in a dozen places, it might not be healthy for Trail's people to make a pass at us. Too obvious. But we've got to do it fast, because they're thinking of stopping us at once. They must be."

"Would you like me to get Dan and Bobby back here so that we can make a plan for first thing in the morning?" Lydia asked.

"You're a doll," Quist said. He lifted a hand to his eyes. "Believe it or not, I'm pooped. While you phone I think I'll try a hot and cold shower. It might revive me."

He went into the bedroom, stripped down, and went into the bathroom. He opened the glass door of the built-in shower and turned on the hot. The needle point spray was steaming. He felt the tight muscles at the back of his neck and across his shoulders begin to relax.

Lydia called to him. "Both boys are on their way," she said.

"Thanks, baby."

"Julian?"

"Yes?"

"Mind if I join you?"

Before he could answer she slid open the glass door and stepped in with him. She wasn't any longer wearing the white sharkskin pantsuit.

The success of any public relations firm depends on its contacts. It needs to be able to get printed stories that will help their clients. It has to have friends on the news services, the daily papers around the country, radio and television. It has to build a reputation for not sending out phony releases that will kick back on the sources that use them. Julian Quist Associates had an impeccable reputation with its outlets. Which is why the decision to take a shot at Trail

Enterprises had to be so carefully thought out.

Colonel Brownlow seemed to be the best takeoff point for a news story.

"He's in just as much trouble as we are," Dan Garvey pointed out. "Why not tell it the way it is? He's heading up a syndicate to buy the *Queen Alexandria*. Nautical museum, all that. Let him give an interview. In the process he will say he doubts the existence of Jeremy Trail."

"And pow!" Quist said, echoing Lieutenant Kreevich.

"Maybe not," Garvey said. "We have the machinery to release that story simultaneously to every major news service in the world. The best reporters for every service and every major newspaper will start checking out. Not just Myra, not just us, but dozens of experts who won't let go of the story until something like the truth turns up. There's a safety factor in it, because nothing can happen to any of us without a big question being asked by a great many people."

"If we make the release, Julian," Bobby Hilliard said, "most of our friends in the news media trust us enough to print the story without waiting to check. Three quarters of our list would go for it, I think."

A tight little smile moved the corners of Quist's mouth. "Does it occur to you, chums, that Trail may very well control some of these sources we count on as friends?"

Garvey brought his fist down on the table. "Not all of them! That just couldn't be."

Quist glanced at his watch. "I'd hoped to hear from the Colonel before this. I don't like to stick his neck out for him without asking him."

"If we don't reach him then we have to stick your neck out, pal," Garvey said. " 'Mr. Julian Quist, famous public relations expert, doubts the existence of Jeremy Trail.' "

"No, Julian!" Lydia said.

"This story should be going out over the wires the first thing in the morning," Garvey said.

70

Quist nodded. "So get to work on it," he said.

Garvey didn't move. "My last objection to the whole damned project," he said, scowling. "We can prepare a release that will go out in a few hours. But it will be twenty-four hours before it can appear in print. If Trail has an in with any of the places we send the story he'll know about it before it appears. I repeat, Myra lasted half a day. If we name the Colonel or you as the rumor spreader—" He shrugged. "There may be a bigger story than the rumor. A second person who had the notion that there is no Trail will wind up in the morgue. That's a bigger story than the rumor itself, chum."

Quist turned away. "So we don't risk the Colonel's neck," he said. "The rumor comes from me. Get to work on it, children."

"Julian, please!" It was a whispered plea from Lydia.

"We have an edge on Myra," Quist said. "We're expecting danger."

At 4 A.M. Colonel Winston Brownlow had still not returned to The Players. Prowling his apartment, Quist felt a faint chill of concern running along his spine.

Lydia, Garvey, and Bobby Hilliard had headed across town to the offices of Julian Quist Associates to prepare the release that was going to go round the world with the light of day. Quist, standing on his terrace, waited for that first light to appear in the east. Something curious had happened to him in the roughly forty-eight hours that had passed since his first luncheon with Colonel Brownlow. At that luncheon the Colonel had seemed to him to be an eccentric old codger. Buying the *Queen Alexandria* had seemed like a quixotic, multi-million-dollar self-indulgence. Attacking the most powerful man in the world hadn't made much more than childish sense, but it had been a provocative idea. But childish. It had hooked Quist. If there was no Jeremy Trail

71

it was a fascinating idea, and maybe the biggest news story since the atom bomb.

The Colonel's dark talk about 'a contract for a hit' had seemed a little too melodramatic to be real, but the possibility of a retaliation against his business had seemed not out of the question to Quist and it had, vaguely, angered him. Nobody should be allowed to have so much power. Something perverse in him had urged him to accept that challenge. But now the vision of Myra Rudolph's body bobbing against the piles of Pier Eighty-nine, and Lieutenant Kreevich's certainty that a cold-blooded murder would be cynically swept under the rug, had raised his temperature to a boiling point. Lydia was right. They were responsible for what had happened to Myra. If Kreevich was right, the proper forces of law-and-order were not going to be able to square Myra's account. Trail's empire would blunt, and divert, until Myra was forgotten. They would even present the police with a solution if it was necessary. All that would be left was Quist, nipping at Trail's heels like an hysterical spaniel. When they got tired of that they would slap him down.

Common sense told Quist to forget it. He didn't have the power, the means, the weapons to fight Trail's empire. Face facts, common sense told him. You're a good golfer, chum, but you can't play Arnold Palmer for money. You're just not that good. You're a good citizen, imbued with righteous anger, but you can't fight City Hall. Let it go, common sense told him. The best you can do is irritate the Trail forces by uncovering a secret they want to keep hidden. The result can only be that they'll turn their guns on you and you'll get yourself flattened, common sense told him. It's an evil world, common sense told him, and little people can't fight the big evil.

A streak of red appeared on the eastern horizon.

"Screw common sense!" Quist said out loud.

He couldn't live with himself or with his world if he turned his back on a violence he had started.

At 6 A.M. Colonel Brownlow still had not returned to The Players, nor had he called in or left any message.

At twenty minutes past six Quist's doorbell rang. Lydia and Garvey were outside. The minute he looked at them Quist knew something unexpected had happened.

"Ball game's over," Garvey said. He handed the morning newspapers to Quist—the *Times* and the *News*. Both papers carried a front page photograph. It was of two men standing together just outside the Ritz Hotel in Paris. The captions were roughly identical.

> British film star Sir Alec Clements and famous financier, Jeremy Trail, outside the Paris Ritz as they prepared to lunch together yesterday.

There was a brief news story to the effect that Clements was hoping to interest Trail in the financing of a new epic. The *Times* explained the use of the photograph on its front page on the grounds that a photograph of "the mystery financier" was a rarity.

"Death of a rumor," Garvey said.

The story in the *News* had a little more detail. Sir Alec Clements, who was flying "to New York tomorrow to accept the New York film critics' award for Best Actor of the Year," was hoping to interest his "old friend, Jeremy Trail" in the production of a new film. Jeremy Trail had been "the money behind Sir Alec's film *Night Flare*, which had won the actor a nomination for an Oscar."

"'Tomorrow' should read 'today,'" Garvey said. "Story is datelined yesterday, you notice. We've checked. Clements is due in at Kennedy at eleven o'clock this morning."

"That seems to put an end to it, doesn't it, Julian?" Lydia asked.

"It's certainly meant to put an end to it," Quist said.

"It's like they'd been reading our minds," Garvey said. "Nobody's going to pay any attention to this release we've prepared. Trail was 'alive, and well, and living in Paris' yesterday."

"If we spread the rumor," Lydia said, "all that will happen is that the news services will check with Sir Alec and that will be that."

"And we will be expected to believe Sir Alec since he's a client of ours," Garvey said.

Quist turned away. "Feel like making some coffee, Lydia?"

"Of course."

Garvey had a brown manila envelope tucked under his arm. "Not much point in your looking at this release," he said. "We can't use it."

Quist stood in the open doors to his terrace, watching the sun creep up over the skyline. "Red in the morning, sailor take warning."

"So face it," Garvey said, his voice angry and hoarse with fatigue. "I know what's cooking with you, Julian. You got to believe this 'no Trail' idea. It feels like truth. Goddamm it, it feels like it to me. But they've sewed us up. We had them off base for a minute, through Myra, and they reacted. But whatever the truth is we're done for now. Alec Clements will laugh at the story for them, and I promise you a dozen other 'old friends' of Trail's will come out of the woodwork if necessary."

"And Myra's killer goes free," Quist said.

"That's cops' business," Garvey said.

"Kreevich has made it clear he doesn't expect to be allowed to get at the truth."

"So the world stinks," Garvey said. "So what's new?"

"We know someone of Trail's killed Myra."

74

"We think it's highly probable, Julian. We don't know it."

Quist turned away from the terrace. "I wonder what the Trail boys have on Alec Clements?" he said. "I wonder where the hell Colonel Brownlow is?"

The answer to Quist's second question came at about what was a normal breakfast time. There was a telephone call from Jack Worthington, the Colonel's Players Club friend.

"Worthington here," the small, acid voice informed Quist. "You did give me your unlisted phone, remember?"

"You've heard from the Colonel?" Quist asked. He and Lydia were surrounding a cold pot of coffee on the terrace.

"Maybe you'd better talk to him," Worthington said.

"Put him on."

"Can't do that," Worthington said. "Not able to come to the phone."

"He's hurt?"

"Not exactly. Think you ought to get down here if you can."

Worthington was waiting at the front door of The Players for Quist.

"Doctor's with him now," Worthington said, "but we're to go up."

"What's wrong with him?" Quist asked.

"Poor jerk has vomited up everything inside him except his own entrails," Worthington said. "Never saw anyone so

76

sick in my life. This is not just an ordinary hangover, Quist. Old boy claims he's been poisoned. Whatever it is, he's wretched." He grinned. "Spelled without the 'w' it makes a pun. Rather good, no?"

"No," Quist said.

They went up four floors in a tiny, creaking elevator with a picture of Sarah Bernhardt on the back wall. Then they climbed a wide stairway, lined with photographs and old playbills dating back to the nineteenth century. Then up a narrow, winding stair, ducking to keep from hitting low beams with their heads, to what was laughingly called the penthouse. It was a pleasant, airy room with a private bath at the very top of the house.

"Firetrap," Worthington muttered as they went in. "Have to jump if the stairwell ever caught."

From the windows Quist saw the green of Gramercy Park. Colonel Brownlow, a great mound of flesh, lay on the bed covered by a sheet. An elderly doctor was putting things back in his medical bag.

"Not much else I can do for him," the doctor said. "Pumped him out. Taking a sample to the lab to see what the hell he took on. Something pretty ghastly."

The Colonel turned his head. His eyes were swollen and blurred. His face looked sunken.

"Oh God!" he said. He turned and fumbled with something on the bedside table. Then he turned back and smiled. His face looked better. He had his teeth in! "Thanks for coming," he said.

"Sending something from the drugstore," the doctor said. "Keep him quiet—if you know how!" He left, and they could hear him struggling down the stairs, muttering profanities.

Quist pulled up a chair beside the bed and prepared to sit.

"Keep the way open to the john," the Colonel said. "When I have to go, God do I have to go!"

Quist moved the chair slightly. "What happened to you?" he asked.

"I was at the party on the *Queen*—as you know," the Colonel said. His voice was weak from what he'd been through. "Good time, talking to old friends. Watching you and the glamorous Sophia. Next thing I knew I was wedged between two garbage cans in a filthy alley, robbed. Money gone, wallet gone, credit cards gone. If anyone had found me they couldn't have identified me. But nobody did find me. Couldn't move. Every bone in my body felt paralyzed."

"Naturally, after fifteen hours," Worthington said.

"Fifteen hours!"

"Last thing he remembers was at about three o'clock," Worthington said. "Next thing he wakes up in the garbage at a little after six this morning. Fifteen hours."

"Hell of a time," the Colonel said. "I'd vomited—while I was out, you understand. I was a filthy mess. I crawled out of the alley. Not anyone around to speak of. I was just a block away from the *Queen*. I could see her. No money for a taxi, even if there'd been a taxi. Every ten yards I had to upchuck—in an alley, in the gutter. First I thought I'd find a policeman who'd help me, but I was sure he'd take me for some rum-soaked bum and throw me in a tank somewhere. I don't know how, but thank God I made it here. Took me two hours to cover thirty blocks."

The Colonel had suffered physically and in damage to his personal pride and dignity.

"You were drinking champagne at the party—and blackout?" Quist asked.

"Oh God, don't mention champagne," the Colonel pleaded. He closed his eyes. "Extraordinary thing," he said. "As you say, I was partying like mad—and I woke up in an alley."

"You don't remember feeling ill, wandering off?"

"Nothing. All laughter and a lovely bottom—and blank."

78

"Lovely bottom?"

"Delightful girl from your office," the Colonel said. "Miss Parmalee, is it? I remember I said to her that I had an urgent impulse to pinch her bottom and I hoped I might do so without incurring her displeasure. At my age, I told her, a pinch is about all I'm good for. She gave me the most engaging smile and suggested that I—'be her guest,' I believe the phrase was."

"And did you become her guest?" Quist asked, controlling his smile.

"Delightful moment," the Colonel said.

"And that's the last thing you remember?"

"Not quite. I remember her going off to collar Horace Van Dine. I remember watching her go with regret. She'd asked me to point out Van Dine and Benjamin Clyde to her. Your instructions, she said. I remember regretting everything there is to regret about growing old. And there am I in an alley, my money gone, everything gone, covered with my own upheaval. Oh God!"

"You couldn't, it would seem, walk off the ship in a trance," Quist said. "If you had been taken ill there in the *Queen*'s dining room you'd have been cared for on the ship. Captain Ligget would have seen to that."

"I know. Tried to figure it out between upchucks," the Colonel said. "Best I can do is that I felt ill, which I don't remember now, and got myself off the ship under my own steam. Wouldn't have wanted friends to see me drunk. I don't get drunk, by God. But perhaps I thought that moment had come. Managed to get off the ship, off the pier, looking for a place to be sick. Maybe I staggered up that alley. Maybe somebody dragged me there, seeing I couldn't defend myself. Robbed me. Took off and left me there, out like a light."

"It's possible," Quist said. "I have a hunch your doctor friend will come up with something interesting from his laboratory. There isn't enough liquor in the world to knock you out for fifteen hours." He frowned. "Has Worthington, here, told you about Myra Rudolph?"

"Frightful business," the Colonel said. "I told you crime was Trail's middle name."

"You don't connect your experience with Trail?"

The Colonel pushed himself up on his elbows. His eyes wide. "Holy Jerusalem!" he said.

"You weren't just sick," Quist said. "Somebody put you out of business. Can you guess why?"

The Colonel let himself drop back on his shoulder blades. "Oh, God, of course! What a damn fool! Of course!"

"You can guess why?"

"Bigwigs from the Whitehall Company were aboard. Game of politics to be played," the Colonel said. "Making me look like a drunken sot wouldn't help my case."

"But you didn't behave like a drunken sot," Quist said. "My people were there till the party broke up. If you'd behaved badly, they'd have mentioned it to me."

"If old George Whitehall saw me passed out and covered with my own filth—" The Colonel shuddered.

"I don't see how you could have gotten off the *Queen* during the party, ill, without being seen by friends. The ship's officers are your friends. The stewards, most of the crew, know you and respect you. There'd have been dozens of helping hands ready the minute you showed signs of being in trouble. You'd have been taken to a cabin somewhere, the ship's doctor sent for. You were in loving hands on that ship, Colonel."

"Some loving hands!" Worthington said. "They fed him some kind of a Mickey Finn, rolled him, and left him to die in a pile of garbage. God save me from that kind of loving hands."

Quist stood up. "Have either of you seen the morning papers?"

"Too busy running," the Colonel said.

"Too busy helping him run," Worthington said.

"Trail's picture on all the front pages," Quist said. "It was taken yesterday outside the Ritz in Paris, in company with Sir Alec Clements, the actor."

"Not possible!" the Colonel said.

"But there it is," Quist said. "By the wildest kind of chance, coincidence, what-have-you, Alec Clements is a client of mine. He's due in at Kennedy Airport in a couple of hours. Like to make a bet with me, Colonel? I'll make you a bet that the minute Clements hits our friendly shores he'll call me for an appointment. It will ostensibly be for the purpose of hiring me to promote his new film, but in the process will be a charming account of his lunch yesterday with Jeremy Trail, his many lunches in the past with Jeremy Trail. He will put an end to your suggestion that Jeremy Trail is a myth."

The Colonel forced himself up on an elbow again. "If you believe him," he said.

Quist nodded. "If I believe him." He bent down and touched the Colonel's clammy hand. "I want to find out what happened to you, Colonel. When you've got your sea legs back, I'd like you to go back to the *Queen* with me and talk to your friends. Someone there must have seen something."

"I'll go now," the Colonel said. He tried to sit up and sweat broke out on his forehead.

"When you've got your strength back; this afternoon, tomorrow morning," Quist said. "I want to be available for Sir Alec Clements when he puts on his Academy Award performance for me."

"So you don't believe him in advance?" the Colonel asked, with a kind of childish eagerness.

"My belief is in a state of suspension, Colonel, but I must say it tips your way," Quist said.

Miss Gloria Chard, the eye-catching receptionist for Julian Quist Associates, was, as usual, delighted to see her employer when he turned up a little before ten.

"I don't have to tell you that there are people churning in the visitors' lounge and that there are messages, all claiming to be urgent," she said.

"Not today, doll," Quist said.

"Are you ever coming back to work?" Miss Chard asked.

"Believe it or not, my pet, I am working like mad at this very moment."

"There is one message—"

"Sorry, doll."

"I have orders to give you this one," Miss Chard said. "Orders from you. If I ever have a call from this one—"

Quist grinned at her. "I've forgotten who she is," he said.

"Mr. Milton Chadwick," Miss Chard said.

"Oh Lord," Quist said.

"I've taken messages from Mr. Chadwick before," Miss Chard said. "This is the first time he ever said 'urgent.'"

Quist frowned. "See if you can get him and put him through," he said.

"No problem. He's at the University Club, waiting for you to call," Miss Chard said.

Quist went through to his office. Miss Parmalee made her quiet appearance. She really wasn't psychic. The moment Quist appeared in the outer office Miss Chard pressed a button.

"How are your bruises?" Quist asked.

"Bruises?"

"I've just left Colonel Brownlow," Quist said.

The corner of Miss Parmalee's mouth quivered. "Nice old goat," she said. "He looked so hungry."

"Pinching you was a big moment in his life. Might have been bigger if someone hadn't slipped him a Mickey Finn a few moments later."

"You're kidding!"

"He's a very sick man, as a matter of fact. Tell you later. I'm expecting a call from Uncle Milton. I'll take it when it comes."

Milton Chadwick was somewhere in his early eighties. He had been a business associate of Quist's father and executor of the senior Quist's estate when he was unhappily killed in a plane crash when Julian and his brother Alan had been in their late teens. The old man, a courtesy uncle, had been the Quists' only family in those trying days. Quist was deeply fond of him and felt guilty that he didn't see him oftener. The old man had long since retired. He lived in a small but elegant apartment on upper Park Avenue, but each morning of his life he took off for the University Club and could be found sitting in one of the big armchairs near the windows overlooking Fifth Avenue. There was an elegant old-worldliness about Uncle Milton. His dark suits, beautifully tailored, belonged in the early nineteen-hundreds. He usually wore a white stock with a diamond tiepin. He never stepped out his front door without a carefully brushed bowler hat. There were a half a dozen priceless paintings in his house, all of them by Victorian artists. He had been a figure of importance in the business world in his prime. It seemed sad to Quist that there was nothing left for him to do but make his journey each morning to the University, watch the Fifth Avenue traffic, exchange a few words with some of the younger club members who were courteous enough to pay their respects, and eventually go home to a lonely dinner, prepared and served by a manservant almost as old as his employer.

The call came through. The old man's voice was clear, yet distant as a cowbell somewhere in the Swiss Alps.

"Sorry to bother you on a busy morning, my boy."

"A pleasure, Uncle Milton."

"I hate to ask it, but would it be possible for you to drop

83

by here?

Quist frowned. "This promises to be a rather trying day, sir."

"Now," the old man said, "before your day really begins?" As if he hadn't heard! "I think you might find it rewarding. Unless, of course, my information is incorrect."

"Your information, sir?"

"I've been led to believe you are interested in a man named Jeremy Trail."

Quist's hand tightened on the receiver. "You know him, sir?"

"Quite well at one time," Uncle Milton said.

"I'll be at the University within fifteen minutes," Quist said.

"Splendid. Be a delight to see you, Julian."

Quist, walking west from his office to the University, told himself he should have known. He could never remember Milton Chadwick asking a favor for himself. The old man was a dispenser, not a receiver.

A uniformed bellman led Quist to the Fifth Avenue windows in the main lounge, to a high-backed armchair of dark green leather. Milton Chadwick, looking like a fragile china doll, held out his hand. On a side table was a slender white coffee cup, a copy of the morning *Times,* and a cigarette in an ivory holder sending a curl of blue smoke up from a silver ash tray.

"A pleasure to see you, Julian."

"The pleasure is mine, sir."

"And how is your brother, Alan?"

"He's not a letter writer, sir. As you know, he teaches at Southern Cal, but in the summertime he nomads it around. I have no idea where he is at the moment."

The bellman had brought up a Windsor armchair which he placed next to Chadwick. Quist sat down and waited, politely, for the old man to speak his piece. Pale, pale eyes

84

looked at Julian as if he expected Julian to begin.

"What do you hear, my boy?"

"Hear, sir? About what?"

"No, no. What do you hear, as we sit here, quietly, not talking?"

Quist turned his head. There was the low murmur of voices from two old gentlemen sitting a few yards away.

"Muffled conversation, sir?"

"Precisely," Uncle Milton said. "For the last twenty years I have sat in this chair every day of my life. My hearing is quite acute for my age. I'm like a piece of the furniture to most people, Julian, an old bit of statuary."

"Nonsense," Quist said.

"I am nonexistent. I'm not alive," Uncle Milton said. He reached for his cigarette holder, flicked the ash from the cigarette into the silver tray, put the holder in his mouth, and inhaled. He looked as if it was one of the very great pleasures on earth. "At my age, Julian, you don't worry about lung cancer. If I were going to get it I'd have gotten it a long time ago." A thin frown appeared between the pale eyes. "At my age you don't worry about dying." The frown cleared. "Do you know what our neighbors are talking about?"

"I'm afraid it's not clear enough for me to distinguish, sir."

The old man looked pleased. "I've learned to tune in, I guess. Those two old gentlemen are discussing whether Tom Seaver is likely to pitch against the Cincinnati Reds at Shea Stadium this afternoon. Now, yesterday, Julian, other people occupied those chairs. I heard the name Trail mentioned. I heard the name Julian Quist mentioned. Well, you can imagine, I rather sat up. A particular phrase came my way—disturbed me. One of the men, a stranger to me, said 'Quist must be turned off.' I was very wide awake then, Julian. The second man, whose name is Horace Van Dine— shipping magnate and a member here—said he quite

85

agreed. 'The Rudolph thing may make that necessary,' Van Dine said."

"What time of day was this, Uncle Milton?"

"About five-thirty in the afternoon. I was about to pull myself together to go home. Of course I had no idea what 'the Rudolph thing' meant until I read this morning's paper. Then the stranger said, 'By tomorrow morning Quist will have no place to go. We're dusting off the Trail image.'"

"'Dusting off?'"

"That's what the man said." Uncle Milton put out his cigarette and picked up the *Times*. "This morning pieces go together," he said. "I had read Myra Rudolph's column yesterday. I was intrigued by her suggestion that Trail is no longer with us."

"May never have been with us," Quist said.

"Oh, he was with us—thirty years ago," Uncle Milton said. "I had daily dealings with him in the early part of World War Two." He pointed at the picture on the first page of the *Times*. "That man is not Jeremy Trail," he said.

Quist looked at the picture for the tenth time that morning. The man standing beside Alec Clements in the picture was wearing black glasses and a soft-brimmed hat that partly obscured his face. "Face isn't very clear," Quist said. "You could be mistaken."

"Nothing to do with the face," Uncle Milton said. "This man is dark, Trail is dark. This man has a straight, hard mouth. Trail has a straight hard mouth. The face—well, I don't go by the face. This actor chap, Alec Clements, is a client of yours, isn't he?"

"How did you know?"

"Recognized your promotional touch when he was being pushed for an Academy Award," the old man said. "One of my few pleasures is guessing who your clients are, Julian, and following their careers. Clements is your man, isn't he?"

"Right."

"How tall would you say he is?"

"Six feet one—two," Quist said.

"Look at this photograph, Julian. Clements is standing beside this man identified as Jeremy Trail. Look closely. They are standing on the same step outside the front door of the Paris Ritz."

"So?"

"This fellow identified as Jeremy Trail is about as tall as Clements, wouldn't you say? Maybe a half inch shorter. But over six feet?"

"Yes."

Uncle Milton leaned back in his chair. "Jeremy Trail is—was—jockey-size, Julian. Five foot two at the most, I'd say. Noticeably small, a tiny man. I don't have to look at the face in this photograph to know that the man in it is not Jeremy Trail."

Quist sat very still, watching the old man. Uncle Milton was not senile.

"In the early days of World War Two I was in the munitions business," Uncle Milton said. "Trail came my way, he and his partner. They had a corner on quantities of scrap metal, a commodity I needed. That was the beginning of his fortune. The shrewdest little operator I ever met. Never knew him to make a wrong decision. Wrong from his point of view, I mean. Everything he touched turned to money. He began to accumulate half the world for himself. A smiling, ingratiating little devil."

"The partner?" Quist asked.

"Not really a partner," Uncle Milton said. "Oh, they started out as partners, but this other chap couldn't keep up with Trail. He became a sort of bodyguard and glorified errand boy. But Trail took care of him. He got rich too, this Italian fellow. Name of Cremona. Tony Cremona. But he was just the tail of the kite. Tough, tough as nails, Cremona. But the business genius was Trail's." The old man shook his head. "This man in the picture is not, could not be Jeremy Trail."

Quist found himself looking around the University Club's lounge. If Uncle Milton could hear distant conversations, he could also be heard.

"Did you ever see a genuine picture of Jeremy Trail in the press, newsreels, any other place, sir?"

The old man stared into a past that must be cluttered with thousands of details of a busy life. "I'm sorry, Julian," he said, "there are some things that don't stick. When I was a youngster I saw Sir Henry Irving act *King Lear* in London. I remember it vividly. But I can't recall if there were pictures of that performance in the newspapers. You have to reject some things from your mental filing cabinets. Not room for everything. But now that you ask, I do recall seeing what purported to be a photograph of Trail, arriving at some airport—or leaving. I remember I doubted at the time that it was really him. That man looked taller, but it could have been a photographic trick. But this one—no doubt. He's standing beside this actor fellow. Trail could change in thirty years, but not grow. Not grow, Julian."

Quist took a cigar from his pocket and lit it. "I value your opinion very highly, sir," he said. "I'd like to tell you where this all started." He outlined Colonel Brownlow's interest in the *Queen Alexandria,* his concern that he would be outbid by Trail, and his suggestion that there really was no 'Jeremy Trail.' Opening that can of peas had evidently cost Myra Rudolph her life, and produced this photograph of a phony Trail in the world press. "Obviously there once was a Jeremy Trail, sir. You knew him."

"Oh, no doubt of that," Uncle Milton said.

"I can see that it might be valuable for some elements in the Trail Empire not to have it known that Jeremy Trail is either dead, or incompetent."

"Trail's sudden death would cause a business panic in

some areas," the old man said.

"So what do you think your strange man meant by 'dusting off' the Trail image?"

The old man fitted a fresh cigarette into his ivory holder. Quist held his lighter for him. "I've been toying with that ever since I saw this photograph at breakfast," the old man said.

"Would you assume that Trail is dead, or incapacitated?"

The old man gave Quist a tight little smile. "I had a quite different thought about it, my boy," he said. "Let us assume that Trail is dead and someone wants to maintain the illusion that he is alive. Someone is engaged to appear in public to stand in for him. Now there must be other people beside myself who know that Trail is a very small man. Why not a very small stand-in? There'd be no problem to get a small man for the job. Why so careless?"

"Interesting point."

"It led me to a speculation," Uncle Milton said. "Jeremy Trail has been built up in the public mind as a man of mystery, a romantic figure. This romantic notion must please a tiny little man. He's probably touchy about his size. He might not be so imposing if people thought of him as jockey-size. So, when there must be a public appearance, there is someone who shows up who will not destroy the romantic image—the dark man of mystery, the man with the beautiful wife, the glittering private and secret world." The old man chuckled. "While the world gets that image to satisfy its romantic soul, a tiny little man sits locked away somewhere controlling human lives; a life and death chess game."

"A fascinating idea," Quist said.

The old man turned slightly in his chair. "I'd appreciate complete frankness from you, my boy. Your interest in this Trail affair—is it simply because it might help your client, this colonel fellow, to expose fraud?"

"It was to start with," Quist said. "Of course it's a wonderful news story if it's true. But it runs a little deeper now, sir. I put Myra Rudolph on to it and she got killed for starting the rumor. I feel responsible. I'm led to believe that the police will be hamstrung. So—"

"So listen to me," Uncle Milton said. "It was Balzac, if I remember correctly, who said that behind every great fortune there is crime. But not careless crime, Julian. Not unnecessary violence. Not and survive exposure for thirty years. Your Miss Rudolph printed a rumor in her column. All they had to do to put an end to that rumor is what they have done: have Trail seen somewhere in public. Why kill her for starting a rumor they can scotch in twenty-four hours? They don't kill from revenge or from anger. They are far too big, too important, too powerful for that."

"Are you suggesting that Myra's death was, in fact, an accident that I should forget about it?"

"No," the old man said. He inhaled deeply on his cigarette. "But if you are right, Julian, and she was murdered, you're missing a piece of the puzzle. Starting that rumor wasn't enough to justify murder. I suggest to you that Miss Rudolph, an energetic and clever newspaper woman, followed up the lead you gave her and stumbled on something they couldn't cover, they couldn't afford to have revealed. What she found is the piece to the puzzle that you're missing, Julian."

"If Myra could stumble on it, so could I," Julian said.

"And wind up where she did," the old man said. He reached out and touched Julian's hand with ice cold fingers. "I urge you to give serious thought to the idea of forgetting about Jeremy Trail. There is, I must assume, very little satisfaction in becoming a dead hero, my boy."

Sir Alec Clements could not appear in public without being mobbed. He was the great romantic figure, the male symbol, the Clark Gable of his time. Teenagers loved him and old ladies loved him. Women of all ages would risk being trampled to death to get his autograph. His disarming smile, his humorously cocked right eyebrow, his graceful movements, turned female knees weak. Even Miss Gloria Chard, Quist's receptionist, accustomed to celebrities and with a rather cynical attitude toward them, felt a faint flutter in sensitive areas, when Sir Alec swept into the office surrounded by a small army of secretaries, bodyguards, and hornblowers. Miss Chard permitted herself the rare privilege of conducting Sir Alec into Quist's office in person, where Quist, Garvey, and Lydia were waiting for him.

"My favorite people in the whole world!" Sir Alec announced. He managed to implant a kiss on Lydia's cheek and to hold out a hand to Quist and Garvey simultaneously. "What luck to find you all together! You all look marvelous, simply marvelous! Oh God, what a madhouse at Kennedy! I didn't think I'd get here with my clothes on."

If Sir Alec noticed that Quist seemed a little quiet and withdrawn he showed no sign of it.

"I've got a new film to top anything I've ever done," Sir Alec said. "And for once, no quibbling about finances. You've seen the morning papers, Julian?"

"I've seen them," Quist said. "I notice you were careful to show the photographer only your left profile, Alec."

"Long training, my dear fellow, long training. The right profile is my character side, the left my romantic side. But what the newspapers didn't tell you is that at luncheon Jeremy agreed to put up ten million dollars, no questions asked. I have it in writing. It's understood that you will handle the entire promotion campaign. Jeremy agreed to that. You are, in his judgment, the very top man in the field. That should make you very happy and someday very rich."

There was a quick exchange of looks between Quist and his people. Sir Alec seemed unaware.

"This may not be the time to discuss it, Julian—the details

I mean. We're a long way from the beginning point of a campaign, but I wanted to be dead sure that nothing will stand in the way of your handling it. Jeremy almost made it a condition for his coming into the deal."

Quist lowered his eyes to the end of his cigar. "You've known Trail a long time, Alec?" he asked.

"Rather longer than I like to remember," Sir Alec said. "I was flying a spitfire in World War Two. Jeremy was helping to supply us with the bullets we shot. Good God, thirty years ago! Don't ever tell anyone that, Julian."

"We all know you're fifty-three, Alec. Prime of life, isn't it, Lydia?"

"For you fortunate males," Lydia said.

"I wish to God you were right," Sir Alec said.

"You're one of the favored few who seem to know Trail personally," Quist said, his eyes opaque.

"Jeremy's a genius in his own way. Has to stay removed from the social whirl or he'd never be able to keep his fingers on the thousand different enterprises he controls."

"But you knew him back in World War Two days?"

"Well. I held down a desk job in the War Office for a bit —recovering from a wound I got in a dogfight over Calais. Jeremy was in and out a lot in those days. We did a little social drinking, a little girl-chasing together." He smiled at Lydia. "We did chase in those days, my dear. There might be no tomorrow, you understand."

"That's what I always say," Lydia said.

"You must have known Trail's partner in those days, too," Quist said.

There was the faintest kind of stiffening in Sir Alec. "Partner?" he asked.

"Little Italian fellow. What was his name?"

"I guess his partner stayed in the background, whoever he was," Sir Alec said. "Jeremy and I did our circulating together—without partners or friends."

Quist leaned forward and knocked the ash off his cigar. "And so yesterday you lunched with Trail and he agreed to come up with ten million dollars?"

"Yes. And when you have a chance to read the film script, Julian, you'll understand why."

"I understand Trail has a phobia about having his picture taken," Quist said. "How did he happen to allow that photograph to be taken yesterday?"

Sir Alec laughed. "He was disturbed at first, but then he was most gracious about it. 'Being photographed is part of your life, Alec,' he said. 'I guess I can stand it this once. I'll be a thousand miles from here tomorrow when that picture appears.'"

"Has he changed much over the years?" Quist asked.

"Jeremy? Oh, we all change, unfortunately. But he's rather remarkable. Power, I guess, does things to one's juices. Still the same old bounce and energy."

"You wouldn't say he'd grown ten or eleven inches over the years, would you, Alec?"

"I don't follow you, old boy."

"You're a great actor, Alec. Under ordinary circumstances I'd have bought your performance a hundred per cent. They hired the right man in you, Alec, but unfortunately you have the wrong audience."

Sir Alec took a white linen handkerchief out of his breast pocket and blotted at his mouth with it. " 'Pon my word, Julian. I don't know what you're talking about," he said.

"Your delightfully casual chitchat doesn't hold water, Alec. If you were a chum of the real Jeremy Trail's thirty years ago, you'll know that he stood exactly five feet two inches tall. The man whose picture was taken with you yesterday is your height. He couldn't possibly have been Jeremy Trail."

"My dear Julian, I—"

"Let's not play games, Alec," Quist said, his voice sharp.

93

"You want to tell me now what the game is I'll keep it as confidential as I can. I understand why Trail may want to stay hidden from the world. If you are a close friend of his, you might be willing to go along with that piece of fakery outside the Ritz yesterday. But here, between us, let's not play games."

Sir Alec's clean physical outlines seemed to sag slightly. "You're not old enough to have known Jeremy thirty years ago, Julian."

"But I know he was a male adult, five feet two inches tall," Quist said.

Sir Alec turned and walked to the windows of the office. His broad shoulders seemed to be shaking. He took a deep, quavering breath and squared them back. He turned and blotted at his mouth once more with the handkerchief.

"Before you improvise something, Alec," Quist said, "let me tell you that I made a bet this morning that you would come here with just the kind of performance you've put on for us. There is a rumor that Jeremy Trail doesn't exist. Someone wants to put an end to it. That photograph of you and someone outside the Ritz was meant to do it. You knew that, Alec, when the picture was being taken. You obviously had instructions to come straight here when you arrived at Kennedy this morning and sew it up with all this intimate crap about a man you don't know. Maybe you were willing in order to get the financing for your film. Curiously enough, I doubt that. You and I have been friends. I don't think you would have willingly tried to hornswoggle me. I won't ask you now, or later, what it is they have on you, Alec. But I do ask you to tell me the truth. You were pressured into this performance, weren't you?"

The churning wheels in Sir Alec Clements's head were almost visible. He looked at Garvey, at Lydia, pleading for help. His voice shook when he spoke. "So far as I know, Julian, the man I was photographed with yesterday is Jer-

94

emy Trail."

"Because the rest of your story is pure invention," Quist said. "You never knew Trail thirty years ago; you never went drinking with him, or girl-chasing thirty years ago. They made it worth your while, only yesterday, to have your picture taken with a complete stranger. They made it worth your while to come here and put on this 'old chum and drinking companion' act with me."

"I have been Trail's guest on many occasions," Sir Alec said. "I have been on trips on his yacht, I've spent time on his island. I know the lovely Sophia—well, you might say intimately. I—"

"But you never laid eyes on Trail himself until yesterday," Quist said.

Sir Alec moistened his lips. "All right, Julian, that is true. I was in his debt for many social pleasures; he offered to finance this new film. So he asked me to tell a—a little white lie about having known him in the old days. He said there was no other purpose behind it than to stop you from spreading an obviously false rumor. Obvious, because there he was!"

"He said."

"Yes!"

"And you had no reason to doubt that the man you were talking to was Jeremy Trail?"

"Why should I?"

"Because you were asked to do a snow job on a friend, Alec. At least I had counted myself as a friend of yours. Let's suppose it was on the level. Trail, to whom you are indebted socially, invites you to lunch because he's interested in financing your film. Financing films is not new with him. You've had dealings with his outfit before. In the process of lunching with him you are photographed together. Perhaps he tells you that he's permitting himself to be photographed in order to squelch an absurd rumor that he doesn't exist.

You both have a hearty laugh over that, drink your martinis, and talk about films. But for some reason they chose to overplay their hand."

"Overplay?"

"You are asked to contact me, refer to the luncheon, and add the false information that you've known Trail intimately for thirty years. They are so anxious, Alec, to turn me off that they put you in a bind to make sure I bought the story. If they'd done nothing but get that photograph published, I might have had to buy. But they overplayed, so I know the whole thing is a phony."

"We also got lucky and found out the truth about Trail's physical size," Garvey said.

"You had to know, the minute they asked you to put on that 'old chum' routine, that the man you were talking to wasn't Trail," Quist said. "You're not a child, Alec."

"I wonder," Sir Alec said, "if I might have a drink?"

"Of course."

"Name it," Garvey said.

"Scotch, neat," Sir Alec said. He walked over to the windows again while Garvey went to the portable bar and made him a drink. Sir Alec accepted an old-fashioned glass filled to the brim with liquor. He drank half of it before he turned back to Quist. "You could, of course, be flimflamming me, Julian. This stuff about a five-foot-two-inch Trail."

"But I'm not."

Sir Alec nodded. "God help me, I believe you," he said. He took another swallow of his drink. "The whole bloody world could come crashing down around my head, Julian, but I'll tell you how it was."

"It's up to you, Alec."

"It was yesterday morning—about eleven. That would be six o'clock New York time, right? I got a call at the hotel I was staying at in Paris from someone who identified himself as Jeremy Trail's private secretary. Would I come to see Mr.

Trail in regard to possible financing for my upcoming film? Well, of course I took off into space. Friends and I have been looking everywhere for money. I knew the Trail Interests had been approached so it didn't seem odd they should be calling. I was given the address of the Middle East Petroleum Company on the Champs Elysées and I went there. I was promptly ushered into a plush private office, and there was Trail. I mean, Julian, there was a man who said he was Trail. We talked about nothing at first, I thanking him for his many hospitalities, my visit to his island, the two trips I'd taken on his yacht. He was most cordial and pleasant. He suggested we lunch at the Ritz and talk about my film.

"We walked to the Ritz together—a few blocks. I was surprised he was so open about it. I had heard he never appeared anywhere openly. On the steps of the hotel we were caught by this photographer chap. I—I tried to brush him off and hustle Trail into the hotel, but he seemed amused. He had no objection to being photographed with me, he said. Now that I think of it, that photographer was planted there, waiting for us."

"Of course."

"So we went in to lunch. He was most agreeable. He said the reason he'd allowed himself to be photographed was that only that morning, in America, a columnist had suggested that he didn't exist. A simple way to end that rumor, he said. We both laughed about it, and then we talked about the film. He had read the script, no doubt of that. He talked about it intelligently. Without any real sales talk from me he consented to put up the necessary funds. I was floating on air. He then asked if it was true that I was leaving for America tomorrow—today, that is. I said I was. I had a commitment to attend the Film Critics' Award Dinner. Then, were you still my public relations man in this country? I said you were. He said complimentary things about you. Then he said that he had reason to believe that you were at the bottom of this rumor about his nonexistence. He said he thought you had been taken in by a client who was out to do him some mischief."

"At least he was very well informed," Quist said.

"Would I drop in to see you when I got here today," Sir Alec went on, "refer to this luncheon and make it quite clear that he did exist. Well, of course I said I would. Be a pleasure, I told him. He seemed awfully real to me, Julian—ten million dollars worth of real! Then things got a trifle odd. He said it was no secret that from time to time he had allowed someone to stand in for him when a public appearance was required. He said you might think that he—the man I was with—was one of those stand-ins. It would help, if I let it drop casually, that I had known him for a long time—back to his beginnings in World War Two when I was an Air Force pilot." Sir Alec finished his drink, and put his glass down hard on Quist's desk. "Well, that was a little sticky, Julian, but—"

"But ten million dollars is ten million dollars," Quist said. "Did you realize then that he had to be a fake?"

"Not really. I thought he was overanxious to prove something to you and I—well, I didn't want to get involved in any dishonesty with you. You were—are—a friend, Julian. I told him I thought I could make you quite satisfied he was real without going into a falsehood."

"And that's when he pulled a knife on you?"

"Knife?"

"Something even more unanswerable than a ten-million-dollar check."

There were little beads of perspiration on Sir Alec's forehead. He blotted at them with the handkerchief.

"That's when he threatened you, Alec, and that's when you knew he was a phony—and you had to do what he said anyway. Right?"

98

"God forgive me, Julian," Sir Alec said. "The knife, as you describe it, is something that could totally destroy me. What I was asked to do to you didn't seem so—so—"

"I'll concede, Alec, that you couldn't know that this rumor they wanted you to help kill had already driven them to one murder," Quist said. He got up and walked away from his desk. Sir Alec watched him, his face washed of its color. Quist turned back to him.

"You are, I suppose, to report back to someone on how effective your performance here was?"

Sir Alec nodded slowly. "I was to pass the word along to Sophia—Mrs. Trail. I really do know her, Julian. Well. The island, the yacht. I think it was because she liked me that the Trail Interests financed *Night Flare*."

"You're to tell her whether you think I bought your story or not?"

"Yes."

"And what will you tell her?"

"Whatever you want me to tell her, Julian. That's the least I can do for you."

"If you care what happens to Julian, tell her he bought it," Garvey said.

Quist seemed to be frozen when he stood. "Tell her I didn't buy it," he said.

"Julian!" Lydia said.

"Tell her the exact truth," Quist said. "That I know the man in the picture with you isn't Trail. That I know you were forced to lie to me. That I'm willing to listen to the truth, but it had damn well better come in a hurry."

"Julian!" Lydia protested again.

"Tell her that to lay off I need a little truth," Quist said.

Sir Alec waited for a moment, as if he hoped someone would change Quist's mind. Then: "If you're sure that's how you want it, Julian."

"I'm sure."

The actor inclined his head in a courteous little bow and walked out of the office. Dan Garvey, watching him, ground out his cigarette in an ash tray.

"You looked at your will lately, Julian?" he asked. "There might be some last-minute changes you'd care to make."

Quist ignored him.

"They killed Myra to stop her from spreading this rumor, Julian. They're giving you the chance to get out of it, stay out of it," Lydia said.

"And I sent Myra to the chopping block," Quist said.

"What are you, some kind of a goddamned boy scout?" Garvey said. "Some kind of St. George trying to kill a dragon? Nobody's going to thank you, Julian. Myra can't, nobody else cares."

"Maybe that's what wrong with the world," Quist said. "Nobody cares." He drew a deep breath and faced his two friends. "There's all kinds of chicanery and crime going on all around us, my pets. In high places and low places. No one of us can be the conscience of the world, but when it happens right on your own doorstep! I couldn't turn my back on some old lady being mugged on the street corner. I could read about it and not start out on a private manhunt, but I couldn't see it and hold still. We sent Myra right to where the muggers were waiting. Now they are saying to us, believe a lie or else. Daniel, Lydia, my dearest of people, I can't turn my back on it. But you two—get out, go away, stay clear of me. I've got a leper's bell around my neck. I think Uncle Milton was right. I think Myra found out something we don't know about yet. Starting the rumor wasn't enough to justify killing her. They could end the rumor just as they did. But if Myra found out something more—well, I've got to know what it was. I can't back off."

Garvey glanced at Lydia. "All right, you stubborn sonofabitch," he said to Quist, "what do you want us to do?"

100

Penny Simmons had been Myra Rudolph's Girl Friday for almost a decade. She was a slim, tense girl who always appeared to be on the run, harried, desperate. Lydia had been convinced that this was part of an act that Penny enjoyed. It added to her importance. Not that Myra hadn't been a difficult person to work for, but while Penny complained of the demands on her that kept her going night and day, Lydia was certain she loved the work and loved Myra.

Penny was in a state of collapse when Lydia appeared at Myra's office that afternoon. Her eyes were red from weeping. The tip of her little pointed nose was red. Her voice sounded as if she'd been strangled by grief. She took one look at Lydia and went off into a bout of convulsive sobbing.

"It's just not possible to believe, Lydia," she finally managed.

"I know, darling."

"She was in such great spirits just before she set out for the party on the *Queen*. I've never seen her so bright, so alive. I couldn't believe it when the police phoned me! I just couldn't believe it! The papers are suggesting that she got

101

tight and fell overboard, but that just can't be true, Lydia. You know that! You know she never drank too much when she was working."

"I know, Penny."

"Each time the phone rings I think it must be some kind of nightmare, and it'll be Myra telling me to do something for her."

"Did she talk to you at all about the item in yesterday's column, Penny? The thing about Jeremy Trail?"

"You gave it to her, day before yesterday over cocktails, didn't you?" Penny said.

"She told you that?"

"Oh, we keep very careful records, just in case," Penny said. "I mean, when someone tips Myra to something, she writes down who it was, when and where it happened, what time—the works. You understand, her business was to hint at things, not say them outright. That's what makes her column so readable. Oh God!" Penny started to wail again. "There isn't g-going t-to b-be any m-more column!" She blew her nose. "In case there was any kickback Myra had to have her sources carefully recorded—in case of legal troubles, you know."

"Well, did she say anything special about the Trail item?"

"Only that you'd put her on to something really hot," Penny said.

"The possibility that Trail was a myth?"

"Hotter than you knew, she said."

"She said that, Penny?"

Penny nodded, wiping at her eyes and her nose with a wet handkerchief.

Lydia tried not to rush it. "When did she tell you that it was hotter than I knew?"

"She stopped in here just before she went to the party on the *Queen Alexandria*," Penny said. "Oh, God, she seemed

102

so—so keen! 'Lydia's put me onto something a lot hotter than she knows,' she said."

"But she didn't say what it was?"

Penny shook her head and pushed tangled hair out of her eyes. "I've only seen her like she was two or three times before, when she was on to something big."

"So big, Penny, that she was killed before she could use what she'd found."

"Oh, God!"

"Penny, what time does her column go to press?"

"Six o'clock at night is the absolute deadline. Usually she has tomorrow's column ready early in the afternoon. But if something happens late—well, she has until six o'clock to add or subtract."

"So what I told her must have been added late," Lydia said. "It was about five o'clock when we separated at the Café Renaissance."

"She phoned it in; dictated it exactly to me," Penny said.

"Was that when she said it was hotter than I knew?"

"No. She just said 'Lydia's given me a fun item,' and dictated the few sentences."

"So it wasn't until the next morning, on her way to the party, that she seemed to think it was something more exciting than she'd first thought?"

"It seemed like that, Lydia."

"Do you have any way of knowing how she spent that evening, Penny, after she left me?"

Penny reached for an appointment pad on what had been Myra's desk. "You're down here for four-thirty," she said. "She was to dine with Reggie Symington at Sardi's at seven-thirty. Reggie is one of her sources, you know. Old blueblood family, no money. She would be buying the dinner, and seven-thirty means they weren't going to the theatre. There's nothing down here for after that, but she almost always went to one of the hot night spots. Reggie would probably know where she was going; may have gone with her."

"Reggie would know the Trail crowd, wouldn't he? Sophia Trail, Neil Patrick, the rest of them?"

"Reggie knows everyone," Penny said.

"Including, possibly, Jeremy Trail?"

"If anyone does you'd guess it would be Reggie," Penny said.

Reggie Symington had been a part of New York's social scene for a great many years. Back in the twenties he had been a young man who attended all the coming-out parties, and was always invited to dances and other occasions as an "extra man." He was invited to the best homes during the summer and winter vacations. He would modestly admit that he couldn't afford to join a party on the Virgin Islands and in the end someone would make him a gift of the trip. A party wouldn't be a party without dear Reggie.

There was a lady who disliked being seen in public without a male escort but whose husband couldn't abide the opera. So for years now Reggie had been visible at the opera each week, both at the old Met and at the new complex at Lincoln Center. The truth about Reggie was that if he had any money at all it was less than enough for his simplest needs. He had lived for forty years now on his charm, his old-world courtesy. Hostesses still thought of Reggie when they were planning something, and there were a few wise and kindly ladies who were aware that as Reggie approached his four-score-and-ten a vague sense of panic was overtaking him. The social picture had changed; the young no longer put great stock by anything old-world Reggie had to offer. These few kindly ladies saw to it that he was invited to lunch or dinner pretty regularly. Dear Reggie mustn't be allowed to starve. But money for an occasional new tie, a new suit, a handkerchief or two to replace the frayed ones in his bureau drawer, cigarettes, subway tokens, was a necessity. Reggie had found a way to earn a little. His conscience bothered him, but he had no choice. He had access to tidbits of gossip. People talked in front of dear Reggie because he was quite safe. He was a sort of zero. Reggie discovered that there was a market for these tidbits—Myra Rudolph and one or two of her sister columnists. He had to be sure that he didn't sell them the same items. He had to be sure that his tidbits had some real meat on the bones. He had to be careful not to be seen too frequently in the company of these gossip purveyors or people might begin to wonder where their information came from. Myra had been the most generous of Reggie's buyers but also the most difficult. She refused to be swept under the rug. She insisted on his appearing in public with her. She insisted on being "friends" with people on the "in." Being seen in public with Reggie did something for her prestige. Reggie tried to persuade Myra to take him to places like Sardi's where they would be more likely to rub elbows with theatre and film celebrities than with the upper-crust social people.

Reggie's last dinner with Myra had been gay, the food excellent, a wine something he hadn't dreamed he would find in Sardi's cellar. Myra had been in very high spirits, but she had been interested in a dangerous topic. Reggie knew better than to mess around with the Jeremy Trail Empire. Myra was insistent. Over the years Reggie must, in all his social wanderings, have crossed Jeremy Trail's past. He must, Myra insisted, have met Jeremy Trail.

There were things Reggie knew about Jeremy Trail that nothing on earth would persuade him to reveal. He wanted, despite the uncertainty of his way of life, to go on living. He tried to satisfy Myra with gossip about the fabulous Sophia. Sophia had, quite openly, been the mistress of Spiros Thanapolis, the multimillionaire Greek shipping magnate. Despite her family background, granddaughter of a royal Italian prince, she had joyfully been a public courtesan. Then Trail had seen her somewhere, met her somewhere, and bought her. Reggie had enjoyed telling that part of it to Myra. It was simply a question that Trail could provide Sophia Pravelli with a hundred times more luxury, more excitement, more power than generous old Spiros. There is very little more in the way of luxury that a billion dollars can buy over against, say, ten million. But power! That was something else, and that, Reggie told Myra, was the lovely Sophia's passion. Power!

Myra had listened to all this impatiently. What about Trail, personally? Surely Reggie had met him somewhere. Reggie tried to satisfy her with bits of gossip about Benjamin Clyde, the lawyer, and Horace Van Dine, the shipping mogul, and Felix Hargrove and others. Myra kept pressing him about Trail. Reggie had felt a little trickle of sweat running down inside his dress shirt. There had been a time when he had been faced with men who thought of killing him. If he ever opened his mouth about Jeremy Trail, that would be the end. So Reggie went on trying to entertain Myra with incidents about the fringes of the Trail empire. That was safe enough. Along the way he mentioned a name, casually enough, and Myra was suddenly excited.

"He is one of Trail's crowd?" she'd asked.

"Always has been," Reggie told her.

This information seemed to delight Myra. She stopped pressuring him about Trail, which was a relief. They finished dinner. Reggie was disappointed when she told him that she had another appointment. He had hoped they might go on to one of the popular night spots.

The next morning he saw Myra's column and wondered what she was up to. He wished she had invited him to the party on the *Queen Alexandria*. There would be hundreds of his friends there he was sure.

106

Reggie spent that day in his miserable one-room apartment. There was nothing on the cards for him until a dinner dance at the Carterets' that evening.

At about five o'clock in the afternoon someone knocked on Reggie's door. Except for the landlord when he was behind in his rent Reggie never had any callers. He was quite honestly ashamed of his poverty. He went to the door, knowing that someone had made a mistake.

He opened the door, and his blood ran cold.

"You!" he said.

The man who faced him had an ugly, angry look to him. "You talk too much, Reggie," he said.

Mrs. Carteret was vaguely surprised that Reggie didn't show up for her dinner dance, but since there were several hundred guests there wasn't time to do much about it. Poor dear Reggie was probably ill.

The next afternoon, after her talk with Penny Simmons, Lydia called Reggie Symington, hoping to talk to him about his evening with Myra. Reggie's phone didn't answer, though it rang and rang. Reggie couldn't answer because he was hanging by his belt from a light fixture in his bathroom. People who knew what a struggle his life had become were not surprised when he was found. The sad old man had committed suicide, it seemed.

That was the way it was meant to seem.

Unable to reach Reggie Symington on the phone, Lydia had tried to check back with Quist. Connie Parmalee reported that Quist had had a phone call from Colonel Brownlow and had gone with their client to the *Queen Alexandria*. Garvey was out, too.

"I haven't had any sleep since I can remember, Connie," Lydia said. "Tell Julian I'll be at my place if he wants me."

"Penny had nothing?" Connie asked.

"Only that Myra seemed to be on to something. She'd had dinner the night before with Reggie Symington, who's a gold mine of malicious gossip. He doesn't answer his home phone, but I'll keep trying him. He just might know what had Myra flying so high."

"Get your sleep," Connie said. "If you've got a number for Symington, I'll keep trying him for you; have him call you if I reach him."

"You're a doll," Lydia said. "I can suddenly hardly keep my eyes open." She gave Connie Symington's number and headed uptown in a cab for her apartment.

The late afternoon sun had turned the city hot and as Lydia stepped into the foyer of her building she was grateful for the cool. She unlocked the front door with her key and went inside. She was startled to see someone sitting on the bottom of the stairway; more startled when she saw who it was.

Neil Patrick stood up, his smile dazzling. He was wearing a pale pink linen suit. He was carrying a bouquet of flowers in one hand and had a bottle of champagne tucked under his other arm.

"I thought you'd never come," he said.

"Well!" Lydia said, not able to think of anything else to say.

He stood very close to her, smiling down at her. She thought she had never seen such bright eyes. "I haven't been able to get you out of my mind, so—I came looking for you," he said. "An English Greek bearing gifts." He held out the flowers and the wine. "You'll have to ask me in."

"How did you get this far?" Lydia asked. She pretended not to see the flowers or the champagne.

"Pressed buttons until someone clicked me in," Patrick said. "This was cold when I brought it," he added, holding out the wine, "but now it needs a little icing to make it drinkable. Shall we provide it with tender care?"

108

"Look, Mr. Patrick, I've had very little sleep in the last twenty-four hours. I was counting on a few hours now. I appreciate the wine and the flowers, but all I can think of is getting some rest."

"It would be fun to watch you sleep," he said, smiling and smiling. "It must be a lovely sight. Then, when you woke up, I would talk to you about what I came to talk to you about."

"Really, Mr. Patrick—"

He interrupted her, laughing. "If you won't invite me in I shall throw myself on the floor, kick and scream, and tell the first person who appears that you attacked me!"

"How absurd!" Lydia said. She had the uncomfortable feeling that this was going to be difficult.

"One glass of wine and five minutes' talk," he said. "My dreams are dishonorable but my behavior will be quite circumspect—if you insist."

"I would certainly insist," she said, aware that she sounded very stuffy.

"Five minutes might not be enough," he said, still smiling, "but in ten minutes I promise you I could persuade you that we were wasting time."

"I think you've gone about as far with this as I care to have you go," Lydia said. "I'm not quite as susceptible as you seem to think, Mr. Patrick."

"I haven't even started to subject you to my personal magic," he said. "However, I must talk to you for five minutes." The laughter went out of his eyes and left them pale and cold. "If you don't choose to invite me in then let me take you to the nearest bar and buy you a drink."

"Some other time, Mr. Patrick. I—"

His hand closed over her wrist and it was cold and strong as steel. "Please don't make me behave like a bully," he said. "Talk to you I must. It can be pleasant or painful. That is for you to choose, Miss Morton."

Her mouth felt dry. "There is a little place just down the block from here," she said.

"Maybe they'll chill the wine for us," Patrick said. "Do let me pin this corsage on your shoulder. Friend or enemy, these little violets should match the color of your eyes perfectly." He was smiling again.

"There's an air of death about her," Colonel Brownlow said. He sounded genuinely moved.

The Colonel and Quist were standing on B Deck of the *Queen Alexandria*, just at the head of the great wide stairway which led down into the main dining room where yesterday people had thronged, laughed, tried to dance to the music, and gotten themselves boiled as owls. It was about four o'clock and the sun was getting low and very hot over the North River. It was just such a day as yesterday had been, clear, cloudless, breathlessly without a breeze of any sort.

Just twenty-four hours ago, Quist thought, Myra Rudolph had been approaching the end of her busy life. Maybe, in the late afternoon of yesterday, she had known the danger that lay ahead of her. If she knew, it must have been a time of terror for her. There were still perhaps two thousand people on the great ship. Someone must have been willing to help her if they'd known of her danger. Perhaps, blessedly for Myra, she hadn't known it was going to happen. The blow that smashed her skull could have come from behind. The rest had happened after she was dead—the fall over the ship's side, the degrading floating about in the garbage-filled river, the rough handling of her body by the seamen who had dragged her up onto Pier Eighty-nine and stood watch while someone called the police. She hadn't heard any of the remarks about the shape of her legs, her breasts, what she might have been like in bed when she was alive.

"The "air of death" the Colonel had mentioned had to do

with his beloved ship.

"Never saw her like this," the Colonel said. "Not even the heyday of her peacetime passenger service was it ever like this."

"Meaning?" Quist asked.

"Never quiet like this," the Colonel said. "Turnaround, you understand. One voyage ended. Troops disembarked in my day, luxury passengers in peacetime. Instantly she was swarming with men cleaning, touching up here and there with paint, loading fresh supplies for the return swing, inspecting, checking out. Never-endingly busy. She just sat there, a queen, submitting. This—this is like an old deserted building with a couple of watchmen hidden away somewhere, picking their teeth." The Colonel blew his nose, loudly. "Starting tomorrow they'll begin to inventory her furnishings, her linens, her works of art, her galley supplies; everything right down to the backgammon sets and the shuffleboard games."

"They'll auction everything when she comes up for sale?"

"Every bloody thing," the Colonel said.

A young seaman came running up the wide stairway. He gave Brownlow a brisk salute. "Mr. Havelock will see you now, Colonel. If you'll follow me—"

The ship's personnel had done a magnificent job of cleaning up the dining room. It was, Quist guessed, pretty well back to normal; a magnificent, graceful room. There was no sign of yesterday's revels.

Mr. Havelock was the chief dining-room steward, the equivalent of a maître d' in a plush onshore restaurant.

"More than that," Colonel Brownlow said when Quist put his thought into words. "Served under me in wartime. Everything stripped down then, you know. We fed fifteen thousand men twice a day. Bert Havelock did the ordering, set up the routines."

The young seaman opened the door of a small office and

111

Quist and Brownlow were greeted by Havelock, looking somehow awkward in an ordinary business suit. Quist remembered him from yesterday, elegant in the dress uniform of the Whitehall Line. They shook hands.

"Been telling Mr. Quist about the old days," the Colonel said. "Give him an idea of what you used to have to order for a round trip, Bert."

Havelock smiled his thin, British smile. "He can read an ordinary list there on the wall, if he cares to, Colonel. But shall I begin, Mr. Quist, with seventy thousand eggs? A little more staggering that than a week's ordering for your flat, I daresay. Twenty thousand pounds of flour; twenty thousand pounds of fresh fish; twenty thousands pounds of choice beef loin; ten thousand pounds of lamb; thousands of chickens and squabs for broiling and roasting; forty thousand pounds of vegetables; fifty-five thousand pounds of potatoes. Give you a general idea, Mr. Quist. All that plus hundreds of smaller lots of things from fruits to smoked fish, gallons of milk and cream, and wine and liquor lists. Thousands of bottles of wine; twenty-four hundred bottles of Scotch whisky alone!"

"To keep on top of that," Brownlow said, "you have to be something more than a good headwaiter!"

"And to ride herd on that dining room, on the lookout for the individual needs of a thousand or more diners!" Quist said. "You have a built-in computer somewhere, Mr. Havelock?"

"I have nearly forty years experience on this and other ships, sir," Havelock said, with a rather nice pride.

"The Colonel and I are counting on your demonstrated powers of observation," Quist said.

"I had a rather rough time, yesterday, Bert," the Colonel said. "You know my habits; drinking habits. Never go overboard."

"Of course not, Colonel."

112

"Well, yesterday; it's unbelievable, Bert. At the party as you know. Having first-class time, though a little sad, if you know what I mean, under the conditions. Saying good-by to the old girl, and all that."

"I understand, sir."

"I could have gone a little further than usual, I suppose. Not impossible."

"If you did, it didn't show, sir," Havelock said.

"Well, thank you, Bert. Now I come to the—"

"Excuse me, Colonel," Quist said. He turned to Havelock. "You were noticing the Colonel, Havelock?"

Havelock frowned. "Well, yes and no, sir. I mean, I had no reason to pay attention to him, knowing him as I do. There were a damned ruddy lot of people at that party who needed watching."

"I know."

"I saw you from time to time, sir," Havelock said to the Colonel. "If anyone suggests that you were out of line at any time, sir—"

"It's rather a rum situation, Bert," the Colonel said. "It was a little after three. I'd just been talking to Mr. Quist's secretary. Charming girl, I might say. I remember her walking away to join Horace Van Dine. And then—well, then, Bert, it was six o'clock in the morning and I was lying in an alley about two blocks down the waterfront from the ship. I'd been dreadfully ill. I was dreadfully ill."

"That was fifteen hours later, Havelock," Quist said.

"Point is, if I was ill, made a spectacle of myself on the ship, I'd have been noticed," the Colonel said. "I couldn't have gone staggering about without some of your men—my friends—coming to my aid, so to speak. It would have been mentioned to you."

"No mention," Havelock said. "Whole thing is hard to believe, sir. If you were ill and left the ship our men at the top of the gangway and on the pier would have noticed."

113

"Except that a great many drunken people were coming and going," Quist said.

"But not the Colonel!" Havelock said, in a shocked voice. "He's an institution to the men on this ship, Mr. Quist."

"One thing, we know, Bert," the Colonel said. "It wasn't just liquor that did me in. Doctor pumped out my stomach when I got to my digs. Poisoned I was. What they call in this country a Mickey Finn."

"That's a stunner, sir!" Havelock said.

"It is, rather."

"The whole day is rather a black one to remember," Havelock said. "Same set of questions been asked me by the police about poor Miss Rudolph. How did she get off the ship without being noticed? How could she have fallen overboard without being noticed? Of course I saw her moving about during the party."

"You knew her?" Quist asked.

"She crossed several times with us," Havelock said. "She often greeted us on our arrival here when we were carrying distinguished passengers. It was her job to interview them. Not just ordinary ship's news, you understand. Famous people. Important people."

"Someone like Jeremy Trail, for instance?" Quist asked, his eyes narrowed.

"Yes, sir."

Quist glanced at Brownlow and back again at Havelock. "What does Trail look like, Havelock?"

"Oh, I haven't the faintest idea, sir. Never laid eyes on him to my knowledge. Mrs. Trail has been with us several times, but not Mr. Trail. I only meant, in answering your question, that it would be a person of Mr. Trail's importance that Miss Rudolph would come to interview."

Quist drew a deep breath. "And there was nothing yesterday, no whisper from any of your staff, that the Colonel was acting peculiarly?"

114

"Nothing, sir." Havelock's scowl deepened. "I don't remember seeing you leave, Colonel. But I do remember being a little disappointed, when it was all over, that you hadn't stopped to say good-by when you left. Captain Ligget mentioned the same thing to me. He was a little ruffled by your not stopping off to see him. Last voyage and all that."

"And of course I would have, Bert, if I'd been all there—which obviously I was not."

"The Captain will be glad of the explanation, sir—as I am myself," Havelock said.

"By God, it would be nice to know what happened to me!" the Colonel muttered.

"To you and to Myra," Quist said. "Both of you well-known to the ship's crew and staff; both of you disappear in the middle of a big party; both of you suffer violence, you, fortunately, to a lesser degree than Myra. Both of you vanish in the middle of a time when anything out of the ordinary would, you'd think, surely be noticed."

"Are you suggesting a connection between the two happenings, sir?" Havelock asked.

Quist hesitated. "It is a coincidence, Havelock, that two people who had no connection with each other—I mean, you had no connection with Myra, did you, Colonel?"

"Good God, no," Brownlow said. "She'd have been a child when I was commandant of the Queen; not a reporter in those days. And I'm not high society, which is her racket."

"So it is a coincidence, Havelock," Quist said, "that two people who had no connection with each other should simply vanish in the middle of a gung-ho party. No one saw them leave; no one saw them in trouble, and God knows each of them was in trouble. Connection? In police procedure criminals have what is known as an M.O.—method of operation. The M.O. in both these cases is alike. Now you see 'em, now you don't."

"As I remarked before, it's a stunner, sir," Havelock said.

"I wonder, Colonel, if we might go over the ground," Quist said. "I'm sure you know the ship well enough to make it unnecessary for Mr. Havelock to spare us his valuable time."

"There is a lot to do to get ready for the sale," Havelock said, "but anything I can do to help, Colonel—"

"Nonsense, Bert," the Colonel said. "I know every nut, bolt, and screw in this old girl."

Quist and the Colonel walked out of the office and into the dining room. It seemed huge with only the two of them standing near the entrance doors. Quist toyed with one of his long cigars, but he didn't light it. Havelock's staff had left the great room spotless after the ravages of the party. A cigar ash would seem like a desecration.

"Let's play games, Colonel," Quist said. "There was a special bar set up at the far end of the room, there. That's where you were standing when I sent Connie over to you to have you point out Van Dine and Clyde to her."

"Right."

"You were feeling no pain then?"

"Pain? Oh, you mean ill. Not at all. And yet—I don't remember much after my delightful little passage with Miss Parmalee. I watched her go over to Van Dine who was talking to some people who were strangers to me, and then I—I—"

"Yes, Colonel?"

"That's when I draw a blank, Quist. That's when it was."

"But you remember what went on before that?"

"Clear as a bell."

"Then you must remember Myra being brought to the bar by Neil Patrick. They were standing only a few feet away from you."

"Rather attractive woman with a fruit salad hat? So that was Myra Rudolph!"

116

"Do you remember seeing them leave the bar?"

The Colonel shook his head. "That was about the time Miss Parmalee joined me. After that—blank."

Quist stood scowling down through the rows of fluted columns to where that temporary bar had been. "While you were involved with Connie's seductive figure, you must have put your drink down." He smiled, faintly. "You would have needed both hands for a proper adventure."

The Colonel flushed. "Could be," he said.

"That was when someone could have slipped that bomb, whatever it was, into your glass. Connie left you, you picked up your glass and drank, and—that was it!"

"By George!"

"Tell me, Colonel, this ship is like home to you. If I suddenly felt ill in my own house, in the middle of a party, instead of making a scene I'd head for the nearest john, or my bedroom."

"I don't remember—"

"It would be instinctive. Whatever they fed you was powerful. It acted at once, and you, feeling it happening to you would subconsciously head for safety—a men's room, maybe your old cabin."

"There's a men's room just off either end of the dining room but I don't think I was ever in either one of them in my life. If I had to go to the john I'd have gone to my own quarters, under normal conditions."

"Where were your quarters?"

"Two flights up, off the Main Deck," the Colonel said.

"Take me there," Quist suggested, "as you would have gone in the old days if you were in trouble."

The Colonel led the way to the far end of the dining room where the bar had been and out a door into a wide corridor. There was a flight of stairs there and they climbed up two deck levels.

"Hard to realize how enormous she is," Quist said.

The Colonel was breathing hard. "To impress people we used to say that if you backed her up against the Empire State Building on Thirty-fourth Street the bow would reach four blocks north to Thirty-eighth Street."

The Colonel paused outside a cabin door and tried it. It was open and they went in.

"I had the cushiest quarters next to the Captain," the Colonel said, "because I had to do a lot of entertaining. This was my sitting room. In there my sleeping quarters."

"Let's have a look."

Quist opened the far door and looked in on a charmingly decorated bedroom, with a door opening into a bath. The whole setup looked as if a cleaning maid had just left it.

"I had a wild idea," Quist said. "That you didn't leave the ship till long after the party was over, the deck watches dismissed. That you might, instinctively, have come up here, thrown yourself down on the bed, and slept for hours. No one would be looking for you; no one would have a reason to search this part of the ship. It wasn't open to the partying public, was it?"

"I think not."

"But if you'd come up here, feeling ill, nobody'd have stopped you. You aren't connected with the ship any more, but there isn't a seaman or a steward who would have prevented your going anywhere you chose. They all knew you."

"So someone may have seen me come here!"

"If you did—and not noticed it. Like Chesterton's postman; not seen because there was no reason to pay you any attention."

"But how did I get to that alley where I came to?"

Quist shrugged. "It's all a guess," he said. "But hours later —in the very early morning—you may have left the ship under your own steam, staggered down the street to that alley, and passed out again."

118

"Where somebody found me and robbed me?"

"Could be." Quist finally lit his cigar. "We'll need to check out with Havelock or whoever is in charge of the cleaning procedures. When was this suite last cleaned? If it was this morning, whoever was involved may remember evidences of your having been here."

"What good does it do us to know all this, if, indeed it's what happened?" the Colonel asked.

"It would at least account, without magic, for your not being seen leaving the ship." Quist turned away. "Is there some kind of garbage-disposal unit on the *Queen?*"

"Garbage disposal?" The Colonel's eyes widened. "Why, of course. Refuse collected and deposited at the stern end of the ship, one level below the open deck. Of course in wartime we never got rid of anything at sea. Submarines or surface raiders would spot floating garbage and know we were in the area. But, yes, there is a unit. Why?"

Quist took a deep drag on his cigar. "I keep wondering how Myra was gotten overboard without anyone seeing her body fall."

"God almighty!" the Colonel said. "But wouldn't there have been evidence of refuse on her clothing?"

"The river is lousy with garbage. That's modern man! The police would have thought it unnatural if her body wasn't filthy."

"Does any of this get us anywhere, Quist?"

"Ways both things could have happened," Quist said, "but no proof that they did."

They walked out onto the Main Deck and down a set of outside stairways to the gangway leading to the dock. There was a watch set at both ends of the gangway, but the Colonel wasn't stopped. On each end he was given a friendly salute and asked no questions about his comings or goings. Nor was Quist questioned, because he was obviously with the Colonel.

119

At the street end of the pier they flagged a taxi.

"Drop you off at your office, if that's where you're going," the Colonel said.

"Thanks."

The old man looked tired. The tour of the ship after his violent sickness had taken its toll. "There are two aspects to my problem, Quist," he said. "My friends and I can make a respectable offer for the *Queen*. We believe that hundreds of thousands of people, including the surviving troops who crossed on her, will be in sympathy with the idea of turning her into a nautical museum. Old George Whitehall, and the directors of the Whitehall Company, have a sense of history. But, blast and damn, they are not in business for their health. So the Trail people can outbid us, no matter what our area of respectability may be. We have no chance, Quist, unless we can convince the Whitehall Company they are dealing with international criminals, or unless we can persuade the Trail people to withdraw from the bidding."

"Trained experts have tried for years to prove the criminal aspects of Trail's empire and failed," Quist said. "It seems unlikely we can manage it in ten days."

"Except that we now have the murder of Miss Rudolph to provide us with possible ammunition," Brownlow said.

"The police don't believe they're going to solve that quickly."

"So our one chance is to get the Trail people to give up bidding for the ship," the Colonel said, his tone urgent. "They obviously don't want the rumor that Trail doesn't exist to be pushed. Exit Miss Rudolph. Enter that fraud who appeared in the newspaper picture with the actor chap. We keep pushing. We spread the rumor, keep the fire hot under it. It's my one chance. Are you with me, Quist, or not?"

Quist looked out the cab window at the jammed crosstown traffic. "I know the man in the picture with Alec Clements is a fraud," he said. "I can prove it if I have to.

But I think Myra may have stumbled on something quite different that they couldn't afford to have known. I don't want her murder brushed under the rug because I'm responsible for having gotten her into trouble. But pushing the rumor? I think I'm about to get the top treatment from the top drawer, which will give me an answer."

"Meaning?"

Quist's smile with mirthless. "I think I'm about to be invited to play Samson to Sophia Trail's Delilah."

Part 3

Miss Gloria Chard didn't delay Quist with any small talk in the reception room, a pleasure she rarely denied herself.

"Connie's loaded for you," was all she said, and pressed Miss Parmalee's warning button.

Quist went straight through to his office. He was tired; he felt an anger smoldering deep down inside him. He was convinced that he was being used by Trail's crowd and he hadn't been able to come up with what would be a gratifying countermeasure.

He knew the look on Connie's face. "Don't tell me, let me guess," he said. "What time did Mrs. Trail call, and where am I asked to meet her?"

Nothing happened to Miss Parmalee's deadpan look of efficiency and never being surprised. "She called at three-fifteen. Could you stop by for a drink between five and six? She is staying in the home of her very dear friend Mrs. Roger C. Loomis at Eighty-sixth Street and Fifth Avenue."

"You may let her know that I'll be there," Quist said.

Miss Parmalee didn't move.

"There's something else?"

"Two something elses, if you can take your mind off Sophia Baby," Miss Parmalee said. "Lieutenant Kreevich of Homicide wants you to call. If you are listening to the radio, you may hear about the suicide of Reginald Symington, old-time society hanger-on. The Lieutenant thinks you may be interested to know that Myra Rudoph spent the last evening of her life with Mr. Symington and that Mr. Symington didn't commit suicide."

Quist stood silent, trying to put it together.

"About three-thirty Lydia called me," Miss Parmalee said. "She was very tired, hadn't had much sleep since who knows when. She was trying to reach a Mr. Reginald Symington on the phone because Myra's secretary had told her that Symington had evidently put Myra on to 'something hot.' I told Lydia to go home and go to bed and I would keep trying to get Mr. Symington for her. I never did get him, because, according to the radio, he was hanging by his belt from a light fixture in his bathroom. I did, finally, get Lieutenant Kreevich on Mr. Symington's line, which is how I happen to have his message for you."

"You let Lydia know all this?"

"That's the second something else," Connie Parmalee said. "Lydia doesn't answer her phone. The phone company says there's nothing wrong with it. I sent Jimmy Rodgers around to try her doorbell. No dice. I don't think she'd have gone away without letting me know where she'd be. I was about to go round and have the superintendent let me in."

"Let's go," Quist said.

Ten minutes later Quist and Connie Parmalee walked into Lydia's apartment. Miss Parmalee showed no surprise at the revelation that Quist had a key to the place. Lydia's apartment consisted of a living room, bedroom, kitchenette, and bath. It was a very feminine, very pleasant kind of place. Quist knew a little something about Lydia's movements that day. The night before had been involved with work at his apartment, forty winks on his couch, an unex-

126

pected shower-bath, and then to the office with Dan Garvey and Bobby Hilliard to prepare a press release that was never used. There'd been a gap in the morning while he'd gone to talk to Colonel Brownlow, recovering from his Mickey Finn. There had been a together point again while Alec Clements played his little drama out, and then they'd gone their separate ways. Lydia would almost certainly have come back here to change before she went out on the town. Yet the place was almost unbelievably neat. He looked in the closet and saw the white pantsuit she'd been wearing the evening before.

Connie came from the kitchen, fighting a smile. She handed a scrawled note to Quist.

Miss Lydia, it read, *I went home before you got back. Hope everything is okay. Lucille.*

"One thing's for sure," Connie said. Lydia hasn't been here since she phoned me. There isn't a pin out of place. No nap she. Lucille did herself proud."

"Do you know where she phoned you from?" Quist asked.

"I gather she was at Myra's office. She was certainly headed for here. This is where I was to call her if I managed to get in touch with Symington."

"She ran into something," Quist said, fighting his uneasiness. "Maybe she did get in touch with Symington."

"He'd been dead for a day, according to Lieutenant Kreevich," Connie said.

Quist glanced at his watch. It was a quarter to five. He had the uncomfortable feeling that nothing in his life at the moment was disconnected from the name Jeremy Trail. He felt a hard little knot growing in the pit of his stomach. If Trail's crowd was messing around with Lydia—!

The residence of Mrs. Roger C. Loomis was one of the last of the old private mansions left in the city. Its majestic front door of wrought iron and oak looked past the Metropolitan Museum into the park. It stood there, daring the modern world to run it down. The elderly Mrs. Loomis still spent her summers in her house in Newport, wondering what the world was coming to when Newport could be invaded by jazz festivals. Money and aristocracy were synonymous with Mrs. Loomis, and so she was more than delighted to make her New York residence, and its staff of servants, available to Mrs. Trail. If anyone had ever told her that Mrs. Trail had once been the mistress of a Greek adventurer, and that Mr. Trail was suspected of having criminal connections, she simply hadn't listened. Mr. Trail was the richest man in the world and that was all the credentials that Mrs. Loomis needed.

Quist rang the front doorbell and waited, wondering. He was presently faced by a uniformed maid. He asked for Mrs. Trail.

"Your name please, sir?" the maid asked.

"Julian Quist."

"Please come in. Mrs. Trail is expecting you."

The wide entrance hall was dark. A huge portrait of some Loomis ancestor that might have been painted by Sargent glowered down at Quist.

"If you'll follow me, sir, I'll take you to Mrs. Trail's private sitting room."

The maid led the way up a wide staircase to the second floor and to a large room overlooking the park. It was not a room that fitted the personality of the exotic Sophia. It was full of knickknacks: china dogs, exquisitely carved sailing vessels encased in small bottles, bits of carved ivory from another century, and heavy brocade drapes and overstuffed chairs covered with the same material. Everything else was polished mahogany. There were more ancestors on dark, old canvases.

Quist heard a ripple of laughter behind him and turned.

128

Sophia Trail was watching him, amused. She was wearing a pale, flesh-colored chiffon housecoat, cut rather low in front. Her skin was a lovely, olive tan. She had on silver sandals, and her toenails were lacquered a bright red. Quist, who was concerned about Lydia, felt the knot in his stomach tighten. Seduction was the wrong approach to him at that moment. The maid stood just behind Sophia.

"If you'll tell Caroline what you'd like to drink, Mr. Quist."

"I think talk is all the stimulating I need, Mrs. Trail."

"Bring Scotch, bourbon, and vodka, Caroline—and the mixings," Sophia said. She came into the room and sat down in the corner of the heavy couch. She glanced around the room. "You almost expect the auctioneer to appear from somewhere," she said. "It must have been magnificent and considered very elegant fifty years ago."

"A little longer ago than that, I imagine," Quist said.

She nodded. "My father's palace in Florence has things in it that date back to the fifteenth century. But they were selected with a taste a good deal more lively than this."

"Shall we get straight to the point, Mrs. Trail," Quist said, his voice cold.

"The point?" She laughed and it was a soft, throaty sound. "My dear Julian—I hope you don't mind my using your first name as I hope you'll use mine—I met you yesterday. I was intrigued."

"I think you are more intrigued by the fact that I haven't fallen for Alec Clements's story," he said.

Her scarlet mouth compressed into a flirtatious pout. "I hoped you wouldn't be angry about it. I wish I knew how you guessed the truth."

"It wasn't a guess," Quist said. "I happen to know, just by chance, that Jeremy Trail is, if he is still alive, a very short man: about five feet two or three inches tall. Knowing that the photograph in this morning's paper had to be a fraud, I knew that Alec's story about knowing that man in the photograph as Jeremy Trail, thirty years ago, had to be a lie. So I knew that Alec had been sent to convince me of something that wasn't so. I wondered why."

She smiled and it was warm and intimate. "Because, my dear Julian, you threatened to be a nuisance."

"How did you know?"

"I won't play games with you, Julian. We'll enjoy our drinks more if neither of us plays games. I wonder if you can understand the kind of world we live in, Julian."

" 'We'?"

"My husband and I." Her smile broadened. "Oh yes, Julian, I have a husband. A most extraordinary husband."

"Tell me about him."

"I intend to, Julian. That is, primarily, why I invited you here." She reached out and took a cigarette from a silver box on a low end-table. Quist held his lighter for her. She smelled like something out of the Arabian Nights, mysterious, exciting. She watched him, he thought, to see how being close to her affected him. It was absurd, out of the dream world of Theda Bara. Yet not funny. You could be overcome by the dark ages. He maneuvered to a place in the room so that the late afternoon light was on her lovely face and he was in the shadow.

"Unless you have lived in the world of extraordinary power and wealth that surrounds my husband, Julian, it's difficult to understand the mechanics of his life."

"Let's admit that I have no personal experience with his kind of life," Quist said.

Her eyes narrowed against the smoke from her cigarette and in that moment Quist thought he saw something beyond beauty, charm, and sexual excitement. There was for that moment a cold shrewdness about her that warned he was dealing with something much more than a gracious messenger for the mysterious man in her life.

130

"You run a successful business, Julian. You are the best man in your field. Would it surprise you if I told you exactly what the gross turnover of Julian Quist Associates was for 1968, 1969, 1970, and 1971? Would it shock you if I told you the exact amount you take out of the business for yourself? If I could tell you what salaries you pay, down to the messenger boy in your mail room?"

"It would surprise me," Quist said, "and it would make it clear to me that you have some kind of stranglehold on my accountant, the only peson who could give you such information. Frankly, I couldn't give you those facts myself."

She gave him a bland smile. "We are able to put our hands on information of that sort the instant we need it; about you, Julian, and about almost anyone else in the world, high and low in the power structure. If we couldn't do that, we would be constantly in danger of somebody setting off a bomb under us when we least expected it. My husband doesn't gamble, Julian. Everything he turns his hand to is a certainty."

"I wonder."

Her lovely, arched eyebrows rose. "Oh?" she said.

"You are going to a great deal of trouble with me," Quist said, "trying to persuade me not to spread a rumor that would evidently be an inconvenience."

She nodded, slowly. "Yes, we are," she said. She was smiling again. "Would you like an accounting of how we got interested in you, Julian?"

"Very much."

"Day before yesterday you had lunch with Colonel Winston Brownlow at a place called Willard's Backyard. How do we know? Well, Colonel Brownlow is of interest to us. As you know we propose to bid for the *Queen Alexandria*. The only obstacle to that is a group, headed by Colonel Brownlow, who want to buy the *Queen* and turn her into a nautical museum. The Colonel's group cannot outbid us."

She smiled. "Nobody can outbid us, Julian. The only way he can hope to succeed is by persuading the Whitehall Company not to sell to us. They are an old-fashioned company with a very conservative code of behavior. They just might be persuaded to refuse the highest bid, for sentimental reasons."

"Sentiment is not a part of your world, I imagine," Quist said.

"No part at all," Sophia said. "So we have been observing the Colonel to see how he would play his hand. You came into the picture in Willard's Backyard day before yesterday. You are a top-flight public relations man. What did the Colonel want of you? You came under observation. Later that afternoon one of your people, Daniel Garvey, asked a question of Felix Hargrove, one of Jeremy's partners, and we knew. The Colonel wanted you to launch the rumor that my husband is nonexistent. We had your whole staff under observation at once and we knew that your lovely Miss Morton had made a suggestion to Myra Rudolph—poor Myra."

"So Myra had to be silenced?" Quist asked, his voice cold.

"She had to be diverted," Sophia said, "but we were a little late. The item appeared in her column. The Fates took a hand on our behalf then, I'm sorry to say. I was fond of Myra. I'm deeply sorry about her accident."

"Accident?"

Sophia's face was extraordinarily innocent. "What else?" she asked. She put out her cigarette and reached for another. Once again he came close to her and held his lighter for her. He retreated into the shadow. She smiled at him as if she knew that he was afraid of her in a sort of way.

"We knew enough about you, Julian, to know that you would feel responsible for what had happened to Myra. It would impel you to spread the rumor we don't want spread. So—"

"So you faked the Paris photograph and used whatever it

is you have on Alec Clements to get him to deliver to me a totally false story."

"Yes, we did," she said.

"And when I didn't buy it you asked me to come here so that you could persuade me in some other way to drop my efforts on Colonel Brownlow's behalf?"

"Yes, I did," she said, smiling.

"Did you ever hear of a man named Reginald Symington?" Quist asked.

"I believe so. Yes, of course I have. An elderly gentleman who lives on the fringes of what is left of old world society. I know about him because I have run across him at parties from time to time, but most immediately because our reports indicated that he dined with Myra at Sardi's Restaurant the night before she died."

"Your intelligence staff is surprisingly good. Have they reported to you that he was murdered about twenty-four hours ago?"

Her lips parted. "I had not heard," she said, very quietly. "How shocking."

"Well, it's nice to know that your intelligence sources are sometimes fallible."

"But awfully good," she said. "Would you like me to tell you who shared your bed with you the night before last?"

A muscle rippled along the line of Quist's jaw. "What are you, Big Sister, the All-Seeing Eye?" he asked.

"I am married to the All-Seeing Eye," she said.

He drew a deep breath. His lungs felt restricted. "So I am watched by a superobserver," he said.

"My husband."

"And the Colonel is out of his mind?"

"Entirely," she said, smiling. "Now let me tell you why we don't simply laugh at this rumor you propose spreading. If there's no truth to it, why are we so concerned that you shouldn't spread it?"

"Please do, because it doesn't make any sense at all. If there is a Jeremy Trail, you should be able to establish it in five minutes and to hell with me and my silly suggestion."

"I told you in the beginning, Julian, that if you haven't lived in our kind of world you can't understand the very delicate mechanics of it." She lit a third cigarette with his help. Her smile, as he held his lighter for her, was completely relaxed. "If you were to become ill, seriously ill, when the word got out people would be distressed because you are an extremely attractive and charming man. They would wish you well, and hope for the best for you. If Jeremy Trail becomes ill, a million people will instantly be panic-stricken. 'What about my Middle East Petroleum stock?' they will ask. There would be a financial upheaval that would instantly affect, not only individuals, but, quite literally, governments. By the time Jeremy Trail recovered from his illness there would have been a disaster. Suggest that he doesn't exist any longer and the disaster would reach catastrophic proportions."

"So all he has to do—if he exists—is to step in front of a television camera and end the whole silly business in five seconds."

"I can't go into details with you, Julian. Let me simply say that for the next ten days or so my husband can't do what you suggest."

"He *is* seriously ill?"

"He simply is not in a position to deny the rumor that you think of spreading. Right now, Julian, only you and your staff know that the picture in this morning's paper is a fake. All is calm, all is bright. The financial world, which waits for the sound of a cough from Jeremy, is laughing nervously, and with relief, at the suggestion that appeared in Myra Rudolph's column. That photograph settled that."

"So it will take you a couple of weeks to shore up your position and avoid catastrophe if the rumor is finally be-

134

lieved?"

"In two weeks we can blow your rumor sky-high, Julian. But not tomorrow or the next day."

"And I should get sensible and take a hard look at what has happened to Myra and Reggie Symington?" Quist asked.

For the first time she seemed a little shaken. "It's absurd to imagine that we had anything to do with those two tragedies."

"At best it's a remarkable coincidence."

She leaned forward and the cigarette she held between her tapering fingers wasn't quite steady. "Let's talk realities, Julian. Your interest in this began with Colonel Brownlow's absurd suggestion. He is your client, and spreading this rumor seemed to be a way to help him. You really couldn't care less what happens to Jeremy or me or any of our people. Unfortunately Myra, a mutual friend whom you interested in the notion, had a tragic accident."

"She was murdered," Quist said.

"That is an absurd and melodramatic notion," Sophia said, impatiently.

"Reggie Symington was murdered."

"What possible interest could we have in Reggie Symington?"

"If I knew the answer to that, I could solve the whole puzzle," Quist said.

"Listen to me, Julian. I'm prepared to make you an offer," she said.

His smile was thin. "Hasn't your brilliant intelligence service told you I'm not likely to be bought?"

"Your interest in this is on behalf of your client," Sophia said. "If you win his game for him, you will have earned your fee. So, in return for forgetting this rumor of yours, suppose I told you that the Trail Interests will drop their concern for the *Queen Alexandria*? They will allow the Col-

135

onel to buy his ship and establish his stupid museum. You
will have accomplished what you set out to do: get the
Queen for Brownlow."

"There's a simple way to settle this," Quist said. "Bring
me face to face with a Jeremy Trail in whom I can believe
and the rumor will blow up in my face. I have a friend who
can help settle the whole issue; who knew your husband
thirty years ago. Really knew him."

"Milton Chadwick," she said, frowning to herself.

"Once more I bow to the efficiency of your intelligence,"
Quist said.

"I can do what you ask, but as I've tried to tell you, not
for another two weeks. If you will wait that long—"

"My client will have lost his precious ship by then."

"I've told you, we'll withdraw."

Quist turned away. Twilight had settled over the Park
outside the screened windows. "I'm in this a great deal
deeper than simply acting as a public relations man for Colonel Brownlow," he said. "I started something that has resulted in two deaths, and might very well have produced a
third—Colonel Brownlow. Without the constitution of an ox
he might have joined Myra and Symington in the city
morgue."

"There ain't no Full Up sign hangin' on the front door of
the morgue," a harsh voice said.

Quist spun around. Standing in the door to the sitting
room was the short, squat figure of Tony Cremona. He was
wearing a loose-fitting seersucker suit, a pink shirt with a
black tie, and white buckskin shoes. Quist could have sworn
the jacket hadn't been properly tailored to conceal a gun
carried in a shoulder holster. The man's dark tan, his very
white teeth, his very bright eyes made him look, somehow,
like an actor in stage make-up. From all accounts—Uncle
Milton's account—he had to be in his late fifties.

"You ain't makin' very good headway, doll," Cremona

136

said to Sophia.

She smiled. "Julian is a very stubborn man, Tony," she said. She looked at Quist. "This is Anthony Cremona, a distant cousin of mine, and a longtime associate of my husband's."

Cremona nodded. It was almost like the dismissal of a very unimportant person. He took a thick cigar out of his pocket, bit off the end, and spit out the tip in the palm of a brown hand. He looked around for some place to dump it and chose Sophia's ash tray.

"So how is Mr. Chadwick?" Cremona asked. He lit his cigar with a gold lighter encrusted with his initials in small diamonds.

"Mr. Chadwick is extraordinarily well for his age," Quist said, "and he still has an extraordinary memory."

"His memory turns out to be a goddam nuisance," Cremona said. He blew a huge cloud of acrid smoke almost directly at Quist. "We're offerin' you the equivalent of fifteen million bucks to keep your nose clean—an ocean liner, for God's sake. Anyone ever offer to hand over an ocean liner to you before, buster?"

"You're not handing it over to me," Quist said. He could feel a pulse throbbing in his neck.

"So I figure old windbag Brownlow will hand over two, maybe three hundred grand to you for a job well done. You don't make a hundred grand a day very often, do you, Quist?"

"I don't think you're helping to make Julian love us, Tony," Sophia said. She was leaning back in the corner of the couch, almost, Quist thought, laughing—not at him but at Cremona.

"I don't give a belch in the wind whether he loves us or not," Cremona said. "You played it nice with him, Sophy; you made him a nice offer. All he does is talk a lot of crap about people getting murdered."

137

Two other men appeared at that moment in the doorway. Quist recognized the amazing aura of health and vitality that Connie Parmalee had mentioned. These two men were probably in their fifties, yet they looked ageless. Sophia introduced Horace Van Dine and Benjamin Clyde. Van Dine was stocky, bull-necked, an elegant fringe of gray at his temples. His light gray tropical worsted suit was beautifully tailored, his pale blue shirt custom-made, his pastel pink tie a thing of beauty. Quist knew clothes. Van Dine had spent a great deal of money on this one outfit. His casual calfskin shoes had probably cost him a hundred dollars.

Clyde, the lawyer, was less tailored, perhaps a little more elegant because of the simpleness of his gray slacks and his pale blue linen jacket. He wore a white button-down shirt and a tie of regimental stripes. His fair hair was sun-bleached to an extent that made it difficult to tell if it was naturally white or blond.

Both men acknowledged the introduction with impeccable courtesy. Van Dine, who was closest to Quist, offered a firm handshake.

"We couldn't help hearing the word 'murder' as we came along the hall," Van Dine said, giving Quist a bright smile. He made it sound as though it was all rather jolly.

"This creep is hintin' around that we got something to do with knockin' off the Rudolph dame and some character named Symington," Cremona said. His black eyes smoldered with anger.

"Not Reggie Symington," Clyde said. "I just heard on the radio that the poor old boy had committed suicide."

"The police think not," Quist said.

"How tragic for the old boy," Clyde said. "I think I hear Caroline bringing us some drinks."

The maid came into the room with a well-stocked tray of drinks and dainty hors d'oeuvres. Everything was very social while Van Dine took orders. Quist still refused. Cre-

138

mona refused. The lawyer, the shipping magnate, and Sophia chose martinis, which Van Dine made. The maid passed the tray of goodies and then left them.

"It's time we took off the kid gloves!" Cremona said, when she had gone.

Benjamin Clyde accepted his martini from Van Dine, nodded in a little salute to Sophia, and sipped. He turned to Quist, his manner most courteous. "I take it Sophia has explained to you why we are so anxious not to have this rumor of yours circulated, Mr. Quist," he said.

"Because you can't produce Trail," Quist said.

"For the time being," Clyde said. "Your martini is perfection as usual, Horace. You won't change your mind, Mr. Quist?"

"No thank you."

"We're like a juggler with several balls in the air, Mr. Quist. If we are thrown off balance, we may drop them all, not just one. Sophia has told you that we are prepared to withdraw from the bidding on the *Queen Alexandria*, which, as I understood it, was your only interest—your client's only interest—in this affair."

"So you've won the ball game, Mr. Quist," Van Dine said, his eyes bright over the rim of his martini glass. "We're already out! There's no point in throwing a beanball at us, just for the fun of it."

Quist stood very straight, very still, facing the curiously glamorous army opposite him.

"I'll say it once," he said. "I had never met Colonel Brownlow until I had lunch with him two days ago. His problem, as he presented it, was that he somehow needed to have the Trail Interests discredited so that the Whitehall Company wouldn't automatically go for the highest bid on the *Queen Alexandria*. Between us, I wasn't interested. My professional talents lie in the area of building people up, not tearing them down. The Colonel amused me by asking me if

I'd 'ever done it upsidedown.' Then he made a tantalizing suggestion to me. He bet me a thousand dollars against my agreement to take him on as a client that I couldn't produce anyone who had ever seen Jeremy Trail in the flesh."

"But that's really rather silly, Mr. Quist," Clyde said. "Here are four of us who know him well. We can produce hundreds of others."

"You people involved with him, who'd naturally want to assure me that Trail exists, didn't count," Quist said. "I just needed to find someone not connected with Trail who had met him, had a drink with him, passed the time of day with him."

"You talked with George Forrest, a Government lawyer, who met him," Van Dine said.

"Again, I take my hat off to your intelligence," Quist said.

"I was present at that meeting," Clyde said.

"Has your intelligence told you that Forrest doesn't believe the man he met at that meeting was Jeremy Trail?"

"You can't mean it!" Clyde said.

"Wrong hands," Quist said. "Your stand-in had hands that were too young for a man of the age Jeremy Trail has to be."

"Sonofabitch!" Cremona muttered, under his breath.

"Your friend, Felix Hargrove, acted as if we'd besmirched his mother's reputation when my friend Garvey asked him if Trail was a myth. Can you understand why I found myself fascinated with what appeared to be a whale of a story—a genuine mystery? Not because of Colonel Brownlow's concerns. My own curiosity wouldn't let me drop it."

"Tough for you," Cremona said.

"Easy, Tony," Clyde said, sharply.

Quist's face was rock-hard. "Still driven by my own curiosity, I had one of my people contact Myra Rudolph. If anyone could force you to come out into the open with the truth, Myra was it. So, she made her move, and she is dead,

140

and there is no doubt in the minds of the police that she was murdered. Your intelligence must have informed you of that. You must have people in high places who have relayed that fact to you. I'm led to believe that old Reggie Symington told her something that supported our theory—that Trail doesn't exist. She and Symington are both dead. Now you have offered to buy me off. I refuse, Mr. Clyde, simply because I want to hear what your next threat will be."

There was a moment of dead silence in the room. Then Van Dine stirred the ice in the glass shaker and refilled his martini glass.

"Threats are the very last resort for us in this situation, Mr. Quist," Benjamin Clyde said.

"So?" Quist said.

There was a silent exchange between Sophia, Clyde, and Van Dine. Cremona might not have been there as far as the others were concerned.

"It must be apparent to you," Clyde said, quietly, "that there are business reasons of enormous importance that make it impossible for us to allow you to upset our apple-cart, Mr. Quist. As things stand at the moment the people who would be disturbed by this rumor are satisfied by the photograph in today's paper. Tomorrow morning there will be an interview with Alec Clements, which will appear in the press, and this will go further to quiet things. We have arranged for Sir Alec to be interviewed tonight on one of the talk shows on radio. He will appear on television on the Today Show tomorrow morning, and we hope on the Johnny Carson Show tomorrow night. Any last remaining damage done by the small item in Myra Rudolph's column will have been dissipated."

"So anything I might choose to do doesn't matter," Quist said. "You've covered all the manholes."

"It would be nice if I thought you would believe that," Clyde said. "If you chose, you could produce your elderly

141

friend Mr. Chadwick, and blow us sky-high. You have a reputation for integrity that the mass media respects. Your Mr. Chadwick, beyond any question, knew Jeremy Trail thirty years ago. He could destroy Alec Clements's story. This would be worse than a rumor. We would be accused of covering up some sort of dark secret. Before we could prove that there was nothing sinister about Jeremy's inability to appear in public at the moment, our roof would cave in. You have us, if Sophia will forgive a vulgarity, by the short hairs, Mr. Quist."

"If that's so, where are we?" Quist asked.

"How would you feel, Julian," Sophia asked, "if you destroyed us and then learned, two weeks later, that there was nothing to your suspicions: that Jeremy does exist? You would have destroyed us and literally hundreds of thousands of other people."

"I have a feeling that you are powerful enough to survive anything," Quist said.

"You can bet your life on that!" Cremona growled.

"I don't like to offer you a bribe, Mr. Quist," Benjamin Clyde said.

"I suggest you don't."

"I can tell you how you might invest some spare capital so that if nothing is done to hurt us you would make a handsome profit in two weeks' time. I would also promise you to introduce you to Jeremy Trail at the end of two weeks' time, and you can bring along your Mr. Chadwick to satisfy you that we aren't playing games with you."

"And I am just to forget that two people have been murdered?"

"My dear fellow, upon my honor, we have nothing to do with those two deaths, murder, suicide, or accident. Upon my honor."

"All this talkin' around the bush don't make no sense,"

142

Cremona exploded. "Maybe we should spell it out for this punk."

"You're really not making it easy for us, Quist," Van Dine said, his bright smile ingratiating. "We offer you a simple, peaceful, practical, profitable out." He spread his hands. "We offer you, in exchange for time, the complete satisfying of your curiosity about Jeremy—which, if you'll forgive my saying so, seems to be a kind of neurosis with you. We are men of solid reputations in the business and social worlds. We tell you that this rumor, invented maliciously by Colonel Brownlow for the sole purpose of getting his way about the *Queen Alexandria,* is pure poppycock. We promise you proof of it in two weeks' time. No one of us here is responsible for the deaths of Myra Rudolph or Reggie Symington. What can you possibly gain by crippling Trail Interests and destroying thousands and thousands of investors in our enterprises? To do so would be an irresponsible action on your part. You can achieve your client's ends, get him his ship. Surely your curiosity can be kept in check for two weeks."

Clyde took the ball. "What more can you ask, Quist? You have no reason to want to damage us. No one in Jeremy Trail's world has done you any harm. As a matter of fact we could do a great deal to be of value to you in the business world. If, at the end of two weeks, you aren't satisfied with the proof we present—" He shrugged. "Then you play the game your way."

"What you're saying is that after two weeks you will have accomplished whatever you're up to and I can't hurt you," Quist said.

"You're not being very reasonable," Van Dine said.

"So let's make him be reasonable," Cremona said. His eyes were burning black caverns. "Go ahead, buster, spread your rumor. To make it stand up you'll have to produce your old crock—Milton Chadwick. Had you thought, Mr.

Bright Boy, that you might not be able to produce your witness? Old men have a way of not wakin' up, without warning. You know what I mean? A guy in his eighties, you know what I mean? And after he didn't make it one morning because you're so goddam curious, and you say to yourself, Tony Cremona is responsible for that so I'll shoot my wad, you don't suddenly have any business no more, could be there's other people beside the old crock you care about might not wake up. You know what I mean?"

"Tony!" Sophia cried out, in a shocked voice.

"So he ain't carryin' no tape recorder!" Cremona said. "Let's take off the gloves and lay it on the line. You keep your big mouth shut, buster, or there's a hole liable to open up under you that'll drop you clean through to China. That's the way it is. My friends here can put it to you nice and polite, but I'm tellin' you the way it is. You see what I mean?"

"You've made it quite clear," Quist said. His face looked chiseled out of rock. He gave Sophia a stiff little bow. "Thank you for a most entertaining interlude."

"Your decision?" Clyde, the lawyer, asked.

"To steal a phrase from the world of politics," Quist said, "I will have to give the matter serious thought."

He turned and walked out of the room and down the wide stairway to the front door.

Around the corner on Madison Avenue Quist went into a drugstore, got himself some dimes, and retired to the phone booth in a back corner of the place. He called his office first and was connected with Connie Parmalee.

"I thought you might have gone home," he said, trying to sound as casual as possible.

"I thought I'd better stay here till I heard from Lydia," Connie said.

"Nothing?"

"Not yet. I take it Sophia Baby didn't eat you alive?"

"I'm not sure," Quist said. His voice sounded suddenly tired. "I don't like the feel of it, Connie."

"Lydia will call when she can."

"I know. Will you stand by for a while?"

"Of course."

"I'll be there in about fifteen minutes. See if you can locate Dan. Tell him I need him in a hurry, no matter what else he's planned."

"I heard Gloria Chard inviting him to her place—for a drink," Connie said, her tone slightly ironic. "I think I can catch him there."

145

"Apologize to Gloria," Quist said. "She's been laying the groundwork for a long time."

"I knew all along I should try false eyelashes," Connie said. "I'll be here, boss."

Without leaving the booth Quist took a small address book from his pocket and checked on a number. He dialed. After a while an ancient male voice answered.

"Mr. Chadwick's residence."

"Regan? This is Mr. Quist."

"Oh, hello, sir," the old voice said. "Nice to hear from you, sir. I'm afraid Mr. Chadwick hasn't got home yet. He leaves the club about six-thirty, planning to dine here at seven-fifteen. He should be here in a few minutes."

Quist frowned. "I don't want to alarm you, Regan."

"Has—has something happened to him, sir?"

"Not that I know of. But tell him, when he gets home, that it's most urgent for him to get in touch with me. I'll be at my office in fifteen minutes. He has the number."

"Yes, sir."

"This may sound melodramatic, Regan, but I don't want him to receive any guests or be persuaded to go anywhere until he's talked with me."

"About guests, sir—"

"Yes?"

"A casual acquaintance from the University Club called Mr. Chadwick just a moment ago. He said he wanted to see Mr. Chadwick about a matter of some importance and that he hadn't been able to reach him at the Club. We both assumed he'd started home and this acquaintance is on his way."

"You know his name, Regan?"

"Oh, yes, sir. He's Mr. Horace Van Dine. His father was a onetime business associate of Mr. Chadwick's."

The knuckles of Quist's hand holding the receiver turned white from a sudden tightening of his grip. "This is awk-

146

ward, Regan," he said. "Don't mention my call unless Mr. Van Dine should try to persuade Mr. Chadwick to go out somewhere with him. In that case tell Mr. Chadwick that I'm on my way and that he's not to leave until I get there. I should make it in ten minutes."

"Yes, sir."

"And make sure, Regan, that Mr. Chadwick doesn't eat or drink anything that you haven't personally prepared. Mr. Van Dine might just try to slip something in a drink. Do you understand?"

"No, sir. But I'll follow your orders."

"Good man. Ten minutes."

It was only seven or eight blocks to the old man's apartment. Quist knew that Horace Van Dine couldn't have had more than a five-minute start on him, even if he'd made his move the instant Quist left the Loomis mansion.

The evening traffic on Madison Avenue was heavy, but after only a moment or so Quist was able to hail an empty cab. The driver grumbled something about Quist's being able to make such a distance faster on foot.

"If you can cut something off the walking time, you might just be in for your largest tip of the day," Quist said.

The driver performed a minor heroism and Quist left him staring goggle-eyed at a five-dollar bill for a one-dollar ride.

An elderly doorman informed Quist that Mr. Chadwick had just now returned home. On the house phone Quist got Regan.

"Mr. Chadwick has only just got here, sir."

"And the other?"

"Yes, sir."

"He's there?"

"Yes, sir."

"On my way up!" Quist said.

The elevator seemed interminably slow. Regan, old and

147

arthritic, opened the front door the moment Quist's finger touched the bell.

"They're in the living room, sir," Regan said, in a stage whisper. "I managed to inform Mr. Chadwick that you—"

"Thank you, Regan."

Quist went down the hall to the living room, so familiar to him over the years. There was a large salmon, old as God, mounted on a board over the mantel. Books, endless books, and a marvelous collection of maps of the Roman Empire in its heyday.

"The salmon I caught some years ago," Uncle Milton was saying to Van Dine. "Unlikely as it may seem to you, Horace, the Romans were slightly before my time. Ah, Julian!"

Van Dine spun around. He was good, Quist thought, very good. His smile was automatic. "Well, Mr. Quist and I just left—the same party," he said to Uncle Milton.

"I'm flattered you should both have thought of me," the old man said. "I usually have a little dry sherry before dinner, but I know you more modern members of today's world insist on damaging your taste buds with something stronger. If you would tell Regan what it is you'd like—?"

"A martini would be fine," Van Dine said.

"I'll join you in a sherry, Uncle Milton."

The old man took a thin platinum pocket watch from his vest. "I dine at seven-fifteen, gentlemen." He looked up at Regan. "What are we having tonight, Regan?"

"Roast pheasant, sir."

"Oh dear," Chadwick said. "A roast pheasant must be eaten precisely when it's done or it dries out and becomes tasteless. I have exactly thirteen minutes to give you, gentlemen."

Quist smiled at Van Dine. "You were here first," he said.

Van Dine was good, very good. A man who is caught with his pants down doesn't ignore the embarrassment, he faces up to it. "Very frankly, I came to talk to you, sir, about

148

Mr. Quist," he said.

"Ah, yes," Uncle Milton said. "I'm not surprised. You are somehow aware that I informed Julian that the picture of Jeremy Trail in this morning's *Times* was not a picture of Jeremy Trail at all. You knew that I might do just that when you discovered, too late, that I might very well have overheard your conversation with a friend in the University Club yesterday afternoon."

Van Dine gave him a courteous nod of acknowledgment. "As always, sir, you are several steps ahead of the pack."

"Which may be the answer," the old man said, drily, "to why I have lived so very long."

"I should never attempt to hide anything from you, sir," Van Dine said. "I think Mr. Quist and I are here for almost the same reason, but not quite. He is here to warn you of danger, and I am here to assure you that there is no danger."

"Someone has threatened to be unpleasant if I should make public my certain knowledge that the man in the *Times* photograph is not Jeremy Trail. Julian is here to warn me of the threat, and you to lull me into believing that no one cares what I do? Ah, Regan, the sherry!"

The houseman passed Van Dine his martini, Quist his sherry, and finally the old man his sherry, accompanied by two small white biscuits.

"The simple truth of the matter is this, Mr. Chadwick," Van Dine said, after he had sipped his martini and smiled his appreciation at old Regan. Uncle Milton interrupted.

"Be good enough, Regan, to notify me three minutes before you are ready to serve the partridge."

"Yes, sir." Regan shuffled off.

"You were saying, Horace?" Uncle Milton asked, blandly.

"You and Mr. Quist are both aware of the basic situation," Van Dine said. "Unhappily for us Mr. Quist acquired himself a client who would like to do us harm, a certain Colonel

Browlow. He made the absurd suggestion to Quist that Jeremy Trail is a nonexistent myth. Quist, amused by the suggestion, made an inquiry or two. By the strangest of coincidences the result was that he came to wonder if Brownlow's suggestion might be true. He passed the suggestion to a newspaperwoman who printed a hint of it in her column. We had to squelch that rumor, and so the stand-in for Jeremy with Alec Clements in Paris. The rumor started by the lady reporter was deflated before it really got off the ground. Unfortunately for us, the lady reporter died, violently. The police think she may have been murdered and thrown overboard from the *Queen Alexandria*. Quist chose to believe that we were responsible for this murder—if it was a murder. Absurd, of course."

"Of course," Uncle Milton said, nibbling a biscuit.

"The next thing that worked against us, Mr. Chadwick, was that you, accidentally, overheard a conversation I had with a friend in the University Club. Quist is like a son to you, so you sent for him to tell him that the man in the picture with Clements was not Jeremy Trail. Now Quist is well stirred up. He proposes to turn loose the rumor once more. It could do us incalculable damage. Mrs. Trail invited him to her house to try to convince him that Jeremy is, indeed, very real, but that for another two weeks he cannot appear in public to put an end to this nonsense, once and for all. Quist," and Van Dine smiled amiably, "is a very stubborn man, and also an angry man—because an acquaintance of his was murdered and he can't convince himself that we weren't responsible. In the course of the discussion one of our partners—I think you know him, sir—Tony Cremona?"

"I know him," Uncle Milton said, reaching for his second biscuit. "Corsican brigand!"

Van Dine chuckled. "Apt description. Well, Tony lost his temper, threatened you, sir. Said you might not wake up tomorrow if Quist planned to use you to give substance to the

150

rumor—which we very much hope that Quist will consider not spreading."

"Cremona was always hot-tempered," Uncle Milton said. His pale eyes looked directly at Van Dine. "And when his temper reached the boiling point he never hesitated to act on impulse."

"In this instance be assured, sir," Van Dine said. "It was just talk. I was certain Quist would warn you about what I assure you was an empty threat. I didn't want you to have a moment's uneasiness about it."

"That's very kind of you, Horace. I shall not give it another thought."

"I hope that you, with your worldly experience, sir, will persuade Quist that to spread this rumor is irresponsible and senseless."

"I'm not sure my influence with Julian is strong enough to carry much weight," the old man said. His pale eyes flickered toward the door. "Oh dear, I'm sorry, gentlemen, but Regan has just signaled me. Not to dine at once would destroy what I know has been a labor of love on his part." He stood up, and took a moment to steady himself. "You might tell your friend Cremona that waking up tomorrow morning is a matter of extreme indifference to me, Horace. I have a feeling, however, that Julian might be concerned, and through him the police. Or does your Corsican friend propose to embark on a campaign of mass murder?"

"Of course not!"

"Well, well. Thank you for dropping by, my dear fellow." The old man turned to Quist. "If you can bear to look at my dinner and not share it, Julian, I'd be pleased if you sat with me for a few minutes."

"Glad to, sir."

Van Dine had no alternative but to leave the field. He did it with good grace.

"May I use your phone, Uncle Milton, while you're settling yourself?" Quist asked.

He called the office and told Connie where he was and why he hadn't appeared. There was no word from Lydia. Garvey had been found "where we thought" and would be there presently.

Uncle Milton was already at his place in the dining room, slowly spooning a cup of consommé, a slice of lemon floating on the surface. He gestured to Quist to sit opposite him, but he didn't speak until he had finished his soup. Then he blotted his lips with a fine linen napkin and leaned back in his chair. He closed his eyes for an instant and the lids were pale blue, paper-thin. He looked very tired, very old. Regan shuffled in and took away the soup cup. Quist sat quite still, fretting internally. Where in God's name was Lydia?

The old man opened his eyes. "I have thought and thought," he said. "It's about all that is left to me—thinking."

"It's a luxury, in this age, to have the time," Quist said.

"I think I would like to use a rather coarse, modern phrase about this situation, Julian. It stinks."

"I agree, sir."

"But it may stink for different reasons than you think, Julian."

"Oh."

That was as far as it went for a moment. Regan brought in a dish with a silver cover which he placed in front of Uncle Milton. He removed the cover. A beautifully browned small bird lay on the plate, resting in a golden gravy, a serving of wild rice, garnished with chopped parsley, and a small paper cup of red currant jelly.

"My dear Regan!" the old man said. "It looks absolutely superb. Do bring Mr. Julian something before he dies of envy."

Regan smiled with pleasure. "I have a slice of cold ham and a split of champagne for Mr. Julian, sir," he said, re-

152

membering his tastes.

"Splendid. Splendid, Regan. Thank you."

The old man tasted his bird and gave a little low moan of pleasure. Regan brought the slice of ham with a little scoop of paprika-sprinkled pot cheese beside it. The split of champagne was perfectly chilled. Quist ate. There was nothing else to do. He watched Uncle Milton with a kind of fascination. The old man dissected his bird with the skill of a surgeon, leaving not a speck of eatable flesh on the carcass.

"Superb, Regan," he said to the hovering manservant, and leaned back in his chair once more.

Regan removed the plates, poured the last of the champagne in Quist's glass. He returned presently with two demitasse cups and a silver coffeepot. He poured. He held a light for Uncle Milton's cigarette. It was the hangover of a childhood discipline that kept an impatient Quist silent. You didn't push Uncle Milton into action if you wanted results.

Uncle Milton took a deep drag on his cigarette through his ivory holder and let the smoke out in a long sigh of satisfaction. "You might almost say I feel like a new man. But I see you are almost twitching with anxiety to be off, Julian. Unfortunately I can only operate one step at a time these days. Small pleasures are most important. By God, Regan knows how to cook a game bird."

"If I seem restless, Uncle Milton, it's because Miss Morton, one of my assistants in this matter, is accountably missing."

"Then I must give you the gist of my thinking, which, of course, you may reject."

"I will certainly listen most attentively, sir."

"I have been an observer of power and greed and corruption all my life, Julian. Horace Van Dine is a nice chap, an able chap, but he has been corrupted by great wealth and a share of great power. His morals may be in question, but not his intelligence. The same goes for all the men who are

153

tied to Jeremy Trail. Take note of what I consider to be an axiom, Julian. They do not make mistakes. They do not leave themselves in vulnerable positions. They would have us believe, Julian, that that is exactly what they have done in this case. They cannot produce Trail when you threaten them with a dangerous rumor. They stupidly held a conversation within my hearing at the University Club yesterday, so that their faked appearance of Trail with the actor fellow was clearly a fraud. 'Dust off the Trail image,' they said. They stumble around, threatening you, threatening me. They turn loose a gun-toting hoodlum promising dire consequences if you and I reveal the truth. They would appear to have made one mistake after another."

"So without Trail they turn clumsy?" Quist suggested.

"Let me tell you an interesting fact that came my way this afternoon, Julian. Came my way because I remembered something and asked some questions. The syndicate that publishes Myra Rudolph's column and circulates it all over the country cannot afford to risk important libel suits. It will probably come as no surprise to you to learn that before any one of Miss Rudolph's columns went to press it was looked over by a lawyer for the publishers. Proper precautions by a careful and completely honest firm. But I think you may be surprised to learn the name of the syndicate's lawyer. He is one Donald Clyde, son of Benjamin Clyde, one of Trail's top legal brains."

"I just left him!" Quist said. "He was part of the party Van Dine mentioned."

"I have no doubt. The point I want to make, Julian, is this. That column of Myra Rudolph's suggesting that Jeremy Trail might be a myth, had to pass through Donald Clyde's hands before it was set up in type. If its appearing was detrimental to Trail interests, all Donald Clyde had to do was blue-pencil it out and inform Myra that it was too risky."

"So he was in a hurry. He missed it."

"Another mistake," Uncle Milton said. "Mistakes right and left. It's out of character I tell you, Julian, out of character."

"Just what are you trying to suggest, sir?" Quist felt the knot tightening in his stomach again.

"Let's go another step with Miss Rudolph," the old man said. "She is a professional gossip. No one takes her too seriously. In the normal course of events they would simply deny her suggestion. Mrs. Trail could have denied it and expressed some outrage at the suggestion that some other man was keeping her young and beautiful. Instead, what do they do? An elaborate fake that they accidentally allow me to know about. No, Julian, before Miss Rudolph came into the picture at all, you were nosing around. Let's take a look at you, Julian. You have a top reputation as a PR man. News sources trust you. If *you* spread the rumor; it could be believed. What do they do? They poison your client. They kill Miss Rudolph—not because of what she printed but because of something she found out along the way. They evidently kill the source of her information, this Symington chap. Then they work on you. At all costs you must *not* set the rumor rolling. What do they know about you, Julian?"

"God knows. They know who I slept with night before last. They know how much I pay my office receptionist and the mail-room boy."

"That's simple espionage, my boy," Uncle Milton said. "I could find out those things if I wanted to. What they know about you is that you're honest, you can't be bought, you feel responsible for what happened to Miss Rudolph, the last thing in the world to do to persuade you to do what they want is to offer to bribe you or to threaten you. Everything they have done so far to keep you from spreading this rumor, which they say threatens them so gravely, has been a mistake. They have handled you all wrong, Julian. They

155

are driving you to do just what they say they don't want you to do."

"It's certainly my inclination," Quist said.

"When you've located your missing girl and you've made quite sure I'm safe you'll blow them sky-high? Right?"

"Yes," Quist said. "Sky-high—with your help. So don't wake up dead tomorrow, please."

"Listen to me, Julian," the old man said, leaning forward in his chair. "There are too many mistakes in this picture. If my premise is correct, and Trail Interests are where they are today because they don't make mistakes, then we have to come to a rather surprising conclusion. You see what it is, of course?"

"Stupidly, no," Quist said, frowning.

"They want you to spread the rumor!" the old man said. "They're doing everything they know how, and quite cleverly, to drive you into spreading the rumor! They've studied you as a human being; they know your strengths and weaknesses. If they pressure you enough you'll turn into a Holy Crusader—and do *exactly what they want you to do!*"

"God!" Quist said. He felt cold inside his clothes. Then he shook his head. "No. I came into the picture by the purest chance, Uncle Milton. Colonel Brownlow had his own ax to grind. It was he who started me on this line. It was the purest chance."

"My dear, gullible boy," Uncle Milton said. "How much do you know about Colonel Brownlow?"

156

CHAPTER THREE

Quist stood at one of his office windows looking down at the carpet of lights spread out below him by the city. In his childhood he had looked at those lights and allowed his imagination to invent all kinds of melodramatic and romantic happenings that were taking place behind them. Tonight there was no pleasure in that game. Somewhere out there, behind one of those lighted windows, or a darkened window, or out toward the glittering surface of the East River was Lydia.

Lydia had not checked in. It was now about eight o'clock.

Dan Garvey was at one of the phones, listening mostly, asking an occasional question in a low, angry-sounding voice. Connie Parmalee sat in her special chair beside Quist's desk, watching him at the window, watching the unconscious clenching and unclenching of his fists.

Finally Garvey hung up the phone and came across the room, carrying a legal pad on which he'd scribbled a collection of notes. Quist turned back from the window. His face was wiped clean of its usual half-amused, ironic look.

"He checks out a dozen ways," Garvey said, referring to his pad. "First lieutenant in a Guards regiment in World

War One; First Battle of the Somme, wounded, hospitalized, decorated, promoted to captain; became a troop transport expert. After that war went into the moving-picture business, business end. Pretty good man, from all accounts, involved with a dozen big successes. Turned down the offer of a big job in Hollywood in its golden days. Full name, by the way, Winston Leffingwell Brownlow."

"Trail involved in movies in those days?" Quist asked. "He seems to be now."

"I asked," Garvey said. "Trail money seems to have been involved in films both here and in England ever since the name first came on the scene. My source doesn't know if there was any Trail money involved in Brownlow films. Could have been, could not have been. Trail himself never appeared openly in his film deals."

"Go ahead."

"Almost twenty years of this," Garvey said. "Popular man, our Brownlow. People liked him. Society barriers began to break down after World War One. Brownlow always at the best houses, visiting the best families for country weekends. He was a success, you understand. Successes are always popular. Not much detail of any consequence over this period; not detail that supports or doesn't support your Uncle Milton's theory."

"So?"

"World War Two," Garvey said. "Re-enlisted. Promptly involved in the massive problem of moving British troops to the continent. Decorated for bravery at Dunkirk. Could have had a cushy desk job for the duration but wanted active duty. Signed on as officer commanding troops in the transport service. Handled runs through the Mediterranean, all the danger spots. Top-flight officer. Finally made military commandant of the *Queen Alexandria*, top job in the service. VIPs of all kinds crossed with him. He got to know big shots in all areas, politics, military and naval, films,

158

journalism. That old bastard knows everyone. No sign of Trail, but if Trail was ever around, your Colonel would have met him, Julian."

"After the war?"

"He was demobilized here, in this country. Some sort of deal he wangled. Became an American citizen. Became business manager for a theatrical producer here in New York, Lance Nichols. Retired a couple of years ago. Lives at The Players."

"Finances?"

"Well off, by all accounts," Garvey said. "You'd think he'd live more elaborately than that attic-penthouse at The Players. But he's enormously gregarious by all accounts, travels a lot, has friends all over the place, particularly in Europe. The Players is just a sort of home base. Probably his time there doesn't add up to more than two or three months a year."

"Women?"

Garvey snorted. "He's seventy-five!"

For the first time Quist smiled, a tight little smile. "You know anybody seventy-five years old, Dan? My father was going strong with the gals at seventy-five."

"And died of a heart attack! !" Garvey said.

"But what a way to go!" Quist said. His smile vanished. "In all this there is no hookup to Trail?"

"Nothing. Not on the surface," Garvey said. He lit a cigarette, scowling at it. "Your aged Mr. Chadwick may be right. They want you to spread the rumor. Brownlow may be their boy and was used to bait the hook for you. So you don't spread the rumor. So they find somebody else. End of game."

"Is it, Daniel?"

"Well, isn't it?"

"Where is Lydia?" Quist asked, his voice suddenly unsteady.

"Julian, we're checking," Garvey said, elaborately patient. "God help her, she's had an accident. She'll turn up in a police or hospital report somewhere. We're praying for her— and for you, pal—that whatever it is will not turn out to be serious."

"You believe that, Daniel?"

Garvey turned away, angrily. "No, goddammit, I don't."

The room was still for a moment. Connie Parmalee watched Quist, anxiety behind the tinted lenses of her granny glasses.

"Lydia represents a kind of insurance for them," Quist said. "If I don't fall for their scheme and spread the rumor, if by any chance I guess the truth and hold off, then they will use Lydia."

"So then you call the cops and blow them that way," Garvey said.

"And Lydia goes out through the garbage-disposal unit on the *Queen Alexandria* as Myra did."

"So, assuming that they want you to spread the rumor and you do spread it, what happens to Lydia then?" Garvey asked.

"She comes home."

"And she tells you what happened to her and you go to the cops and blow them."

Quist shook his head, slowly. "Lydia will have some elaborate explanation. Everything went black. She's been wandering the city in a state of amnesia."

"Not Lydia!" Garvey said.

"Yes, Lydia. Because they will have convinced her that if she doesn't play it their way, I will be instantly eliminated by Mr. Trail's giant fly-swatter. She will lie to me, to the police, to anyone, because she'll be convinced it is the only way to save my life."

Garvey stared at Quist, his dark eyes smoldering. "I don't like to admit it, but you could be right, Julian," he said.

160

"So to hell with it!" Connie Parmalee exploded. "They want you to spread the rumor, spread it. Be done with it. Get Lydia back and accept her phony story. Get out of it the simplest way you can, boss."

"Uncle Milton's theory makes sense," Quist said, "but we can't be absolutely certain he's right."

"Oh, God!" Connie said.

The office door opened and Bobby Hilliard, ambling on his long Jimmy Stewart legs, came into the room.

"Sorry," he said. "Only just got the message. What's up?"

"Connie will give you the rundown on it in a while," Quist said. "Now I have to ask you a question, chum. You suggested I lunch with Colonel Brownlow the other day. How did that come about, Bobby?"

"Dutch Treat Club lunch," Bobby said, promptly. "I found myself sitting next to the Colonel."

"How did that happen?"

"You sit where you find a place," Bobby said. "The Colonel happened to be next to me. We introduced ourselves. I told him about my job. He gave me a dossier on himself, and his interest in the *Queen Alexandria* and her future. It sounded interesting, and when he got talking about the money involved I pricked up my ears. I suggested he needed a good PR man. He said nobody was untouchable by the Trail Interests. I assured him you would not be. Could I arrange for him to meet you?" Bobby shrugged. "I did."

"You think his sitting next to you was accidental?"

"What else? We're both members. We both arrived a little late. We found seats at the back end of the room."

"You had no reason to suspect that his sitting next to you was planned?"

Bobby looked surprised. "No! I mean, God, Julian, if he wanted to sit next to me for a reason he could have arranged it, I suppose. But the thought never occurred to me.

161

We got around to his problem in the most ordinary sort of way."

"Okay, Connie will catch you up," Quist said. He turned to Garvey. "I have to get to the Colonel," he said. "If Uncle Milton is right and Brownlow is part of the Trail machinery, he knows what happened this afternoon. He knows they offered to withdraw from the bidding on the *Queen Alexandria*. If I don't report it to him, he'll know I suspect something. As my client that's good news for him. As my enemy, he'll know I suspect something if I don't tell him."

"And then?" Garvey asked.

Quist's face was hard. "If the Colonel is our enemy, Daniel, then nothing we've learned about what went on aboard the *Queen Alexandria* adds up. The chief steward, Havelock, is his friend. Dozens of other hands on the ship are his friends. They could all be playing his game for him. We've been asking ourselves what Myra could have learned that made it necessary for them to get rid of her. Well, children, I'll tell you what it could have been. Reggie Symington, unaware of any danger in it, happened to tell her that Brownlow is part of the Trail machine. She confronted Brownlow with it, not aware of how dangerous this information was. That it had to be stopped if I was to serve them by spreading the rumor. The *Queen* is Brownlow's to use as he chooses. He has a small army of friends aboard. If he needed help to dispose of Myra, he had it at hand."

Garvey nodded. "Could be." He swore softly. "The old jerk poisoned himself to account for a lot of time he didn't want you to ask about!"

"Could be. So let's go tell him what I think he already knows, Daniel—that Trail won't bid against him for the *Queen*."

"The whole thing about bidding for the ship could be a phony," Garvey said. "It's Trail's money whoever gets her."

"Right."

"You want me to come with you?" Garvey asked.

"I think the time has come, Daniel, when it may not be too safe to play a lone hand in this game."

Garvey's smile was grim. "Glad to be of help," he said.

Quist turned to Connie. He seemed to be slightly more relaxed by the prospect of action. "Get me Colonel Brownlow at The Players, will you, doll?"

Connie moved over to Quist's desk and glanced at the number file. She dialed and was presently asking for Colonel Brownlow. She covered the mouthpiece with her hand. "He's not in," she told Quist.

Quist frowned. "See if Mr. Jack Worthington is there."

Connie asked, nodded, and handed the phone to Quist. After a considerable wait Worthington's crip, rasping voice came over the line. "Worthington here."

"This is Julian Quist, Mr. Worthington."

"Oh, hello. Something up? I gather they told you Brownlow's out."

"Yes. I thought maybe you could tell me where he is. It's rather urgent. I have an offer for him from the Trail Interests."

"So they're softening up, eh? Miserable bastards! Brownlow, feeling much better, decided to go back to his ship to see if he could come any closer to discovering what happened to him yesterday. Imagine you could find him there."

"Thanks a million."

"I don't suppose you'd be willing to tell me what the game is? Naturally, I'm damned curious."

"Afraid I'll have to leave that up to the Colonel," Quist said. "It's his deal to make or not make."

"Naturally. Quite right. Well, good luck."

Quist put down the phone and stood staring at the desk top for a moment. Then he turned to Dan Garvey. "You got that midget lapel camera of yours here in the office?"

"Yes."

163

"Can you get pictures in the kind of light we're likely to encounter on the *Queen*?"

"Not studio portraits, but pictures," Garvey said. "Meet you at the elevators."

Garvey took off. Connie had moved around the desk and she stood by Quist. She put her hand on the sleeve of his coat.

"These people don't play for matches, boss," she said.

"I know."

"If they've got Lydia—"

"They'll use her to make us play dead," Quist said, his voice harsh.

"Does anything matter except getting her back safe?" Connie asked. "Do you really care what their financial games are?"

"We're being used, Miss P.," Quist said. "We're being forced into being partners in some kind of criminal scheme."

"But does anything matter except Lydia?"

"I promise you one thing, kitten," Quist said. "Lydia comes out of this safe and in one piece or I will hang Mrs. Sophia Trail out to dry in Macy's window!" He bent down and kissed Miss Parmalee on the forehead. "See you around," he said.

"I'll be right here if you need me," she called after him.

Quist and Garvey rode a taxi across town toward Pier Ninety-one. Quist was unnaturally quiet. Garvey, who had a deep regard for his friend, watched him, his dark face set in grim lines. He knew, perhaps better than anyone, how Quist was being ripped apart inside over Lydia's disappearance.

"Connie could be right," he said. "Just give up. Do what they want. Learn a painful lesson."

Quist turned his head. The corner of his mouth twitched. "You think I wouldn't if I could be sure it would guarantee Lydia's safety?" he asked. "I can't prove they've got her,

164

Dan. I can do exactly what they want and there's still no certainty they can afford to let her go. Without a shred of proof that they've got her—" He turned his head away. "We've got to get something on them, Dan; something that will give us some leverage."

"What?"

"God only knows. Proof that they murdered Myra; proof that they murdered Symington; proof that Trail exists and make that proof public."

"And your Uncle Milton could be wrong, and all they really want is for you to stop spreading a damaging rumor."

Quist shook his head. "Some instinct tells me that Uncle Milton is right."

"Me too," Garvey said. He adjusted what looked like a tiny button in the lapel of his coat. "So what are we looking for?"

"Proof that Brownlow is a phony; proof that he was part of a conspiracy on board the *Queen* to get rid of Myra. We have to unearth something we can trade for Lydia."

The taxi turned under the West Side Highway ramp and came to a halt at the mouth of Pier Ninety-one. The two men got out.

"God, she's big," Garvey said, looking up at the *Queen*.

They walked down the pier toward the gangway they could see leading up into the hull of the great ship. Two seamen stood at the shore end of the gangway.

"We're looking for Colonel Brownlow," Quist said.

"You got a pass?" one of the men asked.

"Do I need one?"

"Only way we can let you aboard, sir."

"Will you let Colonel Brownlow know we're here, please."

"We can't leave our post, sir. You got to have a pass."

"Where do I get one?" Quist asked, suppressing anger.

"Whitehall Company," the man said, "but you won't be able to manage that till morning."

"You know Colonel Brownlow?" Quist asked.

"Yes, sir."

"Do you know if he's on board?"

"No idea," the man said.

"Now look," Garvey said, "there's some way you can contact a steward or someone on board and get Colonel Brownlow to vouch for us."

"I don't know who you are, Dad," the man said, "but don't start shoving." Then he seemed to freeze.

Quist and Garvey heard someone coming along the pier and turned. The man, approaching briskly, was Captain Ligget. As he came close he recognized Quist.

"Hello, there," he said. "Something I can do for you?"

"We're looking for Colonel Brownlow," Quist said. "We understand he's on the ship, Captain. This is my associate, Dan Garvey."

"Pleasure," Ligget said, and gave Garvey a firm handshake. "These gentlemen are friends," he said to the guard. "Come along with me, Mr. Quist. If the Colonel's aboard we'll find him."

They started up the gangway. From behind Quist heard a long, low whistle. He turned. The two men at the foot of the gangway were standing at attention, motionless. From higher up on the ship came another long whistle, an echo of the first one. Captain Ligget saw the question in Quist's eyes and chuckled.

"Old man's back aboard," he said. "Meaning me, Mr. Quist. That whistle is a waterfront tradition. You walk on a pier anywhere, a stranger, and you'll hear your presence announced the length and breadth of the pier, on and off the ship. Alert. Authority or strangers on the move."

Aboard the *Queen* they took the little elevator up to the main deck and the Captain's quarters. A white-coated steward was already setting out a collection of drink makings on the stretcher table in the Captain's sitting room. Evidently

166

the whistle had alerted him.

"Evening, Knox," the Captain said.

"Evening, sir."

"Would you happen to know if Colonel Brownlow is aboard ship?"

"I believe he is, sir."

"Will you see if you can locate him and tell him that Mr. Quist is here to see him."

"On the double, sir," Knox said. "Shall I wait to break out ice, sir?"

"I'll manage, thank you, Knox," the Captain said. He looked after the disappearing steward with an almost paternal affection. "Been my personal steward on this ship since 1942 when I came aboard as a junior exec. Two men spend the best part of their useful lives together—it's difficult to have it come to an end." The Captain moved over to a small icebox and filled a silver bowl with ice cubes. "Your pleasure, gentlemen?" He approached the liquor table Knox had set up.

"A little later, sir, if that's agreeable. Mr. Garvey and I have work to do."

"Forgive me, then, if I pour myself a spot," Ligget said. He made himself a Scotch without ice and a splash of soda.

Quist waited until the Captain had taken a substantial swig from his glass. "I suppose you will personally look out for a man like Knox, Captain."

"Oh, yes."

"What about the rest of the *Queen*'s personnel, sir? There must be a thousand or more."

"Nearer fifteen hundred," the Captain said. "Whitehall will take care of many of them in their merchant ships. A good many of the older ones will retire and be looking for shore jobs. We have perhaps a hundred men on this trip who are filling in for those old-timers who didn't want to find themselves demobilized, as it were, away from home."

167

"Discipline held up with these new men?"

"Rather better than I feared."

"Where did these fill-ins come from?"

"Whitehall Company. Their agent at Southampton provided them."

Quist took a moment to light one of his thin cigars. "You know, Captain, that I have a concern for what happened to Miss Rudolph here yesterday."

"Bad business," Ligget said, his face darkening.

"And Colonel Brownlow. You'll understand, then, why I've asked you about new men—men you might not necessarily trust. We talked yesterday about the Trail people. If some of these fill-ins were Trail men, it might explain how both these things happened."

"By God!" Ligget said. "Never occurred to me. Makes me feel a little better, I don't mind saying. I've been deeply concerned that men I trusted were covering something."

"Would it be possible for us to get a list of the names of these fill-ins, Captain?"

"Of course—but perhaps not till morning, Mr. Quist. My executive officer, who has those lists in his office safe, is on shore leave until nine o'clock in the morning."

"We'd appreciate the list when it's available," Quist said.

The atmosphere instantly changed as Colonel Brownlow came barging into the cabin. He seemed to have completely recovered his normal, rather extraordinary vigor. "Quist!" he said. "Glad to see you, my dear fellow. You wouldn't be here if something weren't up." He looked inquiringly at Garvey. Quist introduced them.

"All right to talk in front of Captain Ligget?" Quist asked.

"Of course, my boy. Ligget's one of my oldest and best friends." The Colonel gave the Captain's shoulder a cordial pat.

"I spent some time this afternoon," Quist said, "with Mrs. Trail and her army."

168

"Well, now!"

"They're willing to go to quite extraordinary lengths to prevent our going any further with our rumor, Colonel."

"I can imagine."

"They will withdraw from the bidding on the *Queen Alexandria* if we will agree to stop muddying their waters with our rumor about Trail."

"Oh, by God, that's marvelous!" Captain Ligget said.

Quist found himself studying Brownlow closely. What he suspected now, transformed the Colonel into something quite different from the jovial old gentleman with whom he'd lunched three days ago. If Brownlow was part of the Trail picture, then he should believe that Quist wasn't on to anything. If the Colonel was innocent of any connection, he should be delighted.

"Miserable bastards!" the Colonel said, his jowls twitching.

"But this is a great break for you, isn't it, Colonel?" Ligget said.

"Yes—no—God, I don't know," Brownlow said. He took a cigarette from his pocket and lit it with a hand that wasn't too steady. "There's no way to beat them. No way, no way at all."

"What's wrong?" Quist asked.

"Defections in the ranks," the Colonel said.

"What ranks?"

"People who were in on the financing with me. Early this evening I was informed that three key people who were putting up money on my behalf have withdrawn."

"Reason?" Quist asked.

"No reasons that make the slightest goddamned bit of sense," the Colonel said, his voice angry. "You and I know the reason, Quist. Trail has got to them. Without those three men I can't get up enough money to make a respectable bid, with or without opposition from Trail. Sure they

169

offer not to bid against me. Generous. Great. Except that they've maneuvered it so that I can't bid at all. Their offer is meaningless. Unless I can find new money, or get my defaulting friends back on the band wagon—kaput! Oh, you can't beat Trail. I was dreaming when I thought we could. Murder, blackmail; he handles them like a swordsman handles a foil! A flick of the wrist, and, by God, you're dead!"

Quist stared at him in silence. The Colonel's outrage seemed very genuine.

"I came back here to the ship tonight," Brownlow said, "because it appeared to me our only chance lay in pinning the Rudolph murder on them, perhaps the poisoning job they did on me. There are fifty men on this ship who would break an arm for me. Before the night's out they'll have put pressure on every man on this ship, new or old. Someone's bound to crack."

Because he was listening for it the little clicking sound of Garvey's camera seemed loud as a bell toll to Quist, but no one else seemed aware of it.

Knox, the steward, appeared in the doorway. "A friend of Colonel Brownlow's to see him," he said.

Jack Worthington, the Colonel's Players friend, came jauntily into the cabin. He was wearing a beret over his bald head. It gave him an absurdly comic look.

"Couldn't stand the suspense," he said to Brownlow. "Knew you were here; knew Quist had something up his sleeve. What cooks?"

Brownlow introduced him to Captain Ligget and Dan Garvey, and gave him a quick sketch of the situation. Worthington boiled over like a small teakettle.

"So they screw you out of your ship—if you stand aside and take it lying down!" he said. "So destroy them! Spread the rumor, but good! Get Quist's old gentleman friend to make public that the newspaper picture of Trail is a fake. They'll go to any lengths to persuade you not to act. So act,

170

by God! Once you've done it they're down the chute. No reason, no sensible reason, for them to strike back. They'll obviously have their hands full with other problems. Let it hit the fan, Winnie, and while they're squirming maybe you can find some new financing. Don't let 'em push you around any more. Fight back! What can you lose?"

Brownlow looked hungry. He was a man who saw a way to perhaps avert a bitter defeat. "It might work," he said. "Once we've blown it they'll be too busy to bother about us. What do you say, Quist? Will your Mr. Chadwick play along with us?"

Quist felt that tight knot in his stomach. He spoke a little louder than he intended. The clicking of Garvey's camera made him nervous. "I'm sorry, but I can't go along with you," he said.

"Why not?" Worthington shouted at him.

"These people have an extra weapon. One of my people, Lydia Morton, is missing. I have to believe Trail is responsible. It's a weapon that will make me do exactly what they want. They've made it quite clear they want silence from me. I have no choice. I have no choice but to keep Mr. Chadwick silent."

"Miss Morton is—your girl?" Worthington asked.

"Let's say I'll do anything on earth to guarantee her safety," Quist said.

"Sonsofbitches! They're always one step ahead of you," Worthington said. "But you can only fight fire with fire. Put them over the barrel and your girl isn't any use to them as a hostage any more."

Knox reappeared in the cabin door once more.

"An old friend, sir," he said to Ligget.

Quist," he said.

Chadwick came into the cabin, straight as a string, leaning imperceptibly on a blackthorn stick, wearing a high-crowned derby hat, a flower in the buttonhole of his black

171

coat. Behind him, bent and a little breathless, was Regan.

"Hello, Ligget," the old man said. "Nice to see you after some years. Last time I crossed with you was in 1959, I believe."

"This is an unexpected pleasure, sir," Ligget said.

"Hope I'm not intruding, Julian," Uncle Milton said. "I found it rather urgently necessary to see you, and the girl in your office told me you were here."

"I must say you are a surprise, sir," Quist said. "You know Dan Garvey. This is Colonel Brownlow, whom we discussed earlier this evening." He turned to Worthington. "And this is Mr.——"

"Oh, I know Mr. Trail," Uncle Milton said. "How are you, Jeremy? After thirty years you've hardly produced a wrinkle in that baby face of yours."

Colonel Brownlow turned away. There were beads of sweat on his forehead. Dan Garvey, his face dark, altered his position and Quist could detect the clicking of the lapel camera. Worthington—or Trail, if he was Trail—took off his beret, dropped it on the floor, and drop-kicked it across the cabin.

"You meddling old bastard," he said. "All right, boys!"

The door to Ligget's inner cabin opened and Tony Cremona and Neil Patrick, the movie-handsome Neil Patrick, came into the room. Somebody took Knox, the steward, from behind and pulled him away from the main entrance. Quist saw half a dozen seamen clustered outside.

"What's going on here?" Ligget demanded.

"Sorry to take over your private world, Captain," the little man said. He turned venomous eyes Brownlow's way. "You've really screwed this up, Winnie," he said.

"Don't blame the Colonel, Mr. Trail," Quist said bitterly. "He played his hand with real skill, I thought."

"I'm afraid I rather scotched the play, Jeremy," Uncle

Milton said, so cool. "I have such a high regard for your talents that I simply couldn't believe in all the mistakes you were making."

Colonel Brownlow faced Quist. "So you came here tonight, knowing I'd been giving you a great tub full of gobbledygook?"

"Something like that," Quist said. He felt the room spinning slightly around him. Suddenly the whole thing made no sense at all. Uncle Milton was still the dominating figure in the cabin.

"It would seem to be your move, Jeremy," the old man said to the little man. "You seem to have us physically surrounded, so what do you propose to do about us?"

Worthington, or Trail, made an angry gesture which included Cremona and Patrick and Brownlow, and the four men went over into a private huddle just outside the cabin door where the seamen had collected.

Dan Garvey came over to Quist. "I've decided you're not as bright as I thought you were," he said under his breath. "Mr. Chadwick tells you that Jeremy Trail is a small man, five foot two or three, and you have been seeing such a small man hanging around Brownlow, and you don't even raise an eyebrow to wonder about it?"

"I, too, am a touch surprised, Julian," Uncle Milton said. "I mean, two and two—and all that."

Quist's face had turned plaster-pale. "Whatever my shortcomings, it's showdown time," he said. He looked at Captain Ligget, who seemed to be frozen where he stood by the drink table. "Is there any way, Captain, to sound some kind of alarm that would bring the loyal men on board to help us?"

Ligget's face looked as if he was wounded. "I'm sorry, Mr. Quist," he said.

"You, too, Captain?" Quist asked.

"I'm sorry."

Uncle Milton tapped his blackthorn stick against the toe of his shoe. "When that little Napoleon decides to control a situation he controls it," he said. "You may have to give him a very quick answer, Julian. Identifying him has made him uncomfortable and angry, but they still need you for something to have gone to all the trouble of this elaborate staging. And, unfortunately, there is your Miss Morton."

"I've totaled it up," Garvey said. "There are nine or ten of them right here at close range, plus the rest of the ship's company if Captain Ligget wants to play it that way. Tony Cremona, at least, is carrying a gun. I mention this in front of the Captain because we don't have a chance to make any sort of move."

"I think you can only listen to their proposition, Julian, whatever it turns out to be," Uncle Milton said.

Quist seemed to be in something close to a trance. "By the way, what did you come down here to the *Queen* to tell me, Uncle Milton?"

"Ah, yes. Seems rather unimportant now," Uncle Milton said. "Van Dine came back to my apartment after you'd left. He tried to rationalize with me. No use fighting an opponent who outweighs you, can outpunch you. No matter how good you are you're out of your class. Old cliché of the prizefight world. 'A good big man will always defeat a good little man.' He gave me some indirect assurances. Play the game their way and your Miss Morton will be unharmed. She'll be returned to you—after you've done what they want."

"And did he say what they wanted?"

Uncle Milton smiled. "I told him the conclusion we'd reached, Julian; that what they really want is for you to spread the rumor, using your contacts and your best skills. He was surprised we'd seen through them, but he conceded, rather ruefully, that we'd hit on the truth. So there's no doubletalk needed. I thought you should know this, which

174

is why I came, not dreaming that I'd find Trail here." He paused. "What are you thinking, Julian?"

"He's thinking about Lydia, what else?" Garvey said, in a shaken voice. "He's thinking that they can't be trusted from here to there. He's thinking that she may be dead now and that they'll use his simple-minded hope that she isn't to make him play the game their way. He's thinking that this is a miserable, unjust world."

"I'm thinking that I am the damndest idiot who ever drew the breath of life," Quist said. "A sentimental fool. Tell those clowns out there to come back in here and we'll deal the hand."

"Think carefully, Julian," Uncle Milton said. "Don't let your outrage and anger jeopardize your safety and the safety of your Miss Morton."

Quist turned on the old man, his face carved out of rock. "My safety?" he said. He seemed to Garvey to have gone mad. He grabbed the blackthorn stick out of Uncle Milton's hand and tossed it to Garvey. "That may come in handy, Daniel," he said. His teeth were bared in a frightening grin. The old man had staggered slightly, and now Quist twisted one frail arm behind his back and the old man cried out. Quist's left arm hooked itself around Uncle Milton's neck. He half dragged the old man so that he was standing with his own back to the cabin wall, Uncle Milton in front of him, a sort of shield.

"Brownlow!" Captain Ligget shouted.

"You gone crazy, pal?" Garvey asked.

"Just keep that other old creep off me," Quist said, nodding toward the dumfounded Regan.

"Julian! Uncle Milton said, in a choked voice.

Worthington, Cremona, Patrick, and Brownlow came charging in from the outside corridor. Tony Cremona was tugging at his holstered gun.

"Hold it right where you are!" Quist shouted at them.

175

"Come one step closer and I'll break this old bastard's spindling neck before you can count to one!"

"He's off his rocker!" Cremona said. But his hand came slowly away from the hidden holster.

"I may not be as bright as you thought I was, Daniel, but I didn't overlook that little five-foot-three-inch baldheaded creep. When this fine gentleman whose neck I may break told me Trail was a sort of midget, I wondered about Mr. Jack Worthington. Not hard. He's a member of The Players, an actors' and artists' club. Thirty years ago Mr. Jack Worthington was a pretty well-known vaudeville performer—jokes and soft-shoe routines. When vaudeville died, he turned into a writer for television comics. He made himself a pile and retired a few years ago. He couldn't be Trail. He couldn't possibly be Trail. I didn't mention it to you, Daniel, because I thought you'd laugh at me for suspecting every five-foot-three-inch queer I passed on the street. But I checked out on Mr. Jack Worthington. It must have given you a thrill to pretend to be the most powerful man in the world, Worthington. But now you'd better get down on your knees and pray."

"Let's take him!" Neil Patrick said.

"You'd better ask the Great Man if that's the way he wants it," Quist said. "He's probably made future plans for anyone who doesn't do exactly as he says."

Patrick looked at Uncle Milton. The old man was struggling feebly against the iron arm around his neck.

"Loosen up on him a little, buster. He's tryin' to tell you somethin'!" Cremona said.

Quist's arm relaxed ever so slightly. The old man choked and coughed and then said: "Thank you, Julian. I think I was about to pass out, which might have been awkward for you. So, my boy, you have stumbled into a beehive, you know. You have terms? Because of course we have terms."

"Yes, I have terms," Quist said. "Before anything else

176

Lydia Morton will be brought to this cabin, safe and unharmed."

"Just by chance, that could be arranged," Uncle Milton said.

"You will turn over to the police the murderer of Myra Rudolph, whom I suspect was Colonel Brownlow."

"That might be negotiated."

"Not negotiated, Uncle Milton."

Brownlow laughed, and there was a note of hysteria to it.

"Is there more, Julian?" Uncle Milton asked.

"Yes. You will order Captain Ligget to call Lieutenant Kreevich of the New York police and tell him to get here with enough men to get us off this ship alive—in case you meet my other terms."

"All in all, rather reasonable," Uncle Milton said. "Don't you think you might remove your arm from my neck and we can discuss this like civilized human beings?"

"You've taught me how civilized you are, sir, tonight," Quist said. "We stay exactly where we are till all my terms are met. Your skinny neck is our one chance of coming out of this whole."

"You can't give him what he asks for, Mr. Chadwick!" Cremona said.

"Would you like to change places with me, Anthony?" the old man asked. "I think we might begin by letting Julian see that his lady love is quite unharmed—so far. Neil, will you do the honors? I trust you've gotten to know the lady's ways in the last few hours."

Neil Patrick grinned at Quist and walked out of the cabin.

"Do ease up just a little on my neck, Julian, will you? I shall have a dreadful sore throat in the morning."

"If there is another morning for you, Uncle Milton," Quist said. "But I forget, you've always said you had no fear of dying."

"Not the eventuality, Julian. But I must admit I don't relish the process. About Brownlow—"

"Yes?"

"I really can't turn him in, Julian. He's been a very good man down through the years."

"I daresay you've thrown a thousand other 'good men' to the wolves over the years, Uncle Milton."

"It seems a pity," Uncle Milton said. "He carried out his orders rather well. It was bad luck that Myra Rudolph happened to ask old Reggie Symington about him, and Symington knew that Brownlow had been working for Jeremy Trail for years. When she confronted Brownlow with it at the party on the ship, he had no choice but to—to remove her from the scene."

"He asked her to go somewhere for a quiet chat, and clobbered her with a belaying pin," Quist said.

"A regrettable necessity, Julian."

"And deposited her dead body in the garbage-disposal unit?"

"Unpleasant but efficient." Uncle Milton sighed. "And not the end, unfortunately. Reggie Symington had to be permanently silenced. You, or perhaps the police, Julian, would have discovered that Symington had been the source of Myra Rudolph's dangerous knowledge and what it was."

"The story of the Mickey Finn was invented to account for a long period of time for which the Colonel would have no explanation—the time he needed to find Symington and silence him?"

"You and the police will have to work that out," Uncle Milton said. "I don't propose to give you Brownlow on a silver platter, Julian. Too old a friend."

"If Dan and Lydia and I walk out of here alive, you can't help yourself, Uncle Milton. And if we don't—well, you will be dead before I am so you'll never know what happens. You were the one who arranged to have me involved in all this, weren't you?"

"Why of course, Julian. I knew your talents, your reputation. We wanted the rumor spread that Jeremy Trail doesn't exist. It happens to be the truth. If your conscience matters, you wouldn't have been spreading a lie. But we wanted you to believe it—so that you'd do your very best job, and angry enough at being pushed around to top it with whipped cream. As to what it was all about, that I'm afraid you wouldn't understand, even if there were time to explain it to you. Panic, a wild selling of certain securities on the exchange, a buying-up at panic levels, by ourselves of course, and millions of dollars into preferred pockets. The rumor had to come from an unimpeachable source. You were ideal for our purposes. I was certain I could control your behavior, your thinking, once things got under way. Without the unhappy mischance of Myra Rudolph it would have worked."

"And why try to sell me here that Worthington was Trail?"

"Thought you might be more easily persuaded if you thought you were dealing with the top man. It was worth a try, Julian."

"How was I supposed to read what you were up to?" Quist asked. "First Brownlow tips me off, then I am threatened and Lydia kidnapped, apparently to stop me from going ahead. Then you, the big brain, convince me that they are really trying to get me to do what they pretend they don't want me to do. Then you turn up here and try to palm off Jack Worthington on me as Trail, which puts an end to the rumor—keeps me, in theory, from doing what you've been trying, backhandedly, to persuade me to do. Seesaw, Marjorie Daw! What the hell are you up to?"

"Early this evening sources abroad indicated the need for a change in plans. A military coup in the Middle East has brought about a change in governments. It was suddenly the wrong moment to spread the rumor, Julian. I had to stop you from doing what I had so carefully planned that you would do."

"This morning spreading the rumor would have made you a fortune; tonight the timing was wrong?" Julian asked.

"There were two ways to stop you, Julian, and stop you we had to. We could kill you, the simplest and quickest solution. But I am genuinely fond of you, my boy. Also there were too many people in your office who might have been motivated, by your death, to spread the rumor anyway. They had to be kept silent too, and you were the only person who could turn them off. So, I thought if I showed you Jeremy Trail—someone you could believe was Trail—it would put an end to things. Worthington had a nice little scene to play for you. Too bad he won't be able to show us how good he is as an actor."

"And in case I didn't buy your charade there was Lydia!"

"Never put all your eggs in one basket, Julian. There must always be more than one way to accomplish an end. As for your young lady—"

Quist, looking past the old man's head toward the cabin door, saw Lydia, and his heart jammed hard against his ribs. Neil Patrick brought her into the room, holding on to one arm firmly. Her violet eyes were wide.

"Are you all right, love?" Quist asked.

"Do you mean have I been hurt—or raped? I'm all right, Julian. But—"

"Let her go!" Quist said to Patrick. "Let her go if you don't want me to snap this pipestem neck!"

"Do let her go, Neil," the old man said.

"And now, Captain Ligget, if you'll be good enough to call Lieutenant Kreevich at police headquarters."

Quist thought Lydia had never looked so beautiful as she came uncertainly toward him in her canary-colored dress.

It was hours later. Quist, returning from police headquarters to his apartment, saw Lydia waiting for him on the terrace. The first gray light of dawn was showing in the east. She rose to meet him and he took her in his arms and held her very close without speaking.

"I'm so sorry, Julian," she said, finally. "You were fond of him, weren't you?"

"Very. I—I grew up, thinking of him as a beloved father substitute."

"What will happen to him?"

"God knows," Quist said. "He will have the best legal talent there is to defend him. I don't know exactly what they have on him, in a legal sense. In any case it will drag on and on, probably longer than he can expect to live. Brownlow's goose is cooked. Neil Patrick will be charged with abducting you. The rest? Who knows?" He laughed, a short, bitter laugh. "It's hard to believe that a great financial and, possibly, criminal empire has been operated from a leather chair in the Fifth Avenue window of the University Club!"

"Was he—is he married to Sophia?" Lydia asked.

"She is just part of the whole false front," Quist said. "You know, I believe there once was a Jeremy Trail, a shrewd character selling scrap iron at the outbreak of World War Two, dealing with Uncle Milton. What happened to him, God only knows—God and Uncle Milton. Anyway, Uncle Milton took over, built on what Trail had started, and hid for thirty years behind Trail's identity." He looked down at Lydia. "Was it very rough for you, my sweet?"

She told him about finding Neil Patrick waiting for her, their starting down the street toward a little place she knew for a drink.

"The minute we were out on the street he made it quite clear to me that I had to go with him if I cared about your safety," she said. "He took me straight to the ship." She smiled. "The bridal suite."

"And then?"

"Oh, I was offered the once-in-a-lifetime chance of mak-

181

ing love to Mr. Neil Patrick."

"And—?"

She touched his cheek with her cool fingers. "Until I'm not wanted, whatever I have to give is saved up for you, darling. He told me, quite frankly, that I would probably regret it for the rest of my life."

"Jerk!"

Lydia walked slowly into the living room. She looked back at Quist, smiled, and stepped out of her canary-colored skirt, leaving it where it fell. At the bedroom door she slipped off her blouse and dropped it.

"Julian?"

"Yes?" He turned to look at her, and his troubled frown faded.

"Follow the yellow brick road," she suggested, and disappeared.